A Wind Named
Anne

Books by J. Allan Bosworth

For Young People

A BIRD FOR PETER

VOICES IN THE MEADOW

WHITE WATER, STILL WATER

ALL THE DARK PLACES

A WIND NAMED ANNE

Novels

SPEED DEMON

THE LONG WAY NORTH

A Wind Named Anne

J. ALLAN BOSWORTH

DOUBLEDAY & COMPANY, INC.

GARDEN CITY, NEW YORK

First Edition

Library of Congress Catalog Card Number 74-97652
Copyright © 1970 by Doubleday & Company, Inc.
All Rights Reserved
Printed in the United States of America

A Wind Named
Anne

CHAPTER 1

A fog was gathering when Kip James moved the dory across the lobster bed to the farthest of the bobbing marker buoys. It curled around the jutting tower of Nancy's Light, and like a hesitant wraith, slowly came across the dunes and rocks of the spit and into Podquit Bay. Kip felt its approaching chill, tasted rather than saw the change in late-afternoon air; he hauled in the wicker pots, but his mind was elsewhere.

For weeks, someone had been robbing several of those pots nearest the old lighthouse. It did not happen every day. On this August afternoon, three of the pots in question bore good-sized lobsters. But it had occurred often enough to be almost routine, and he could not come to that part of the bed without wondering who was doing it and why.

Kip baited the pots with chunks of stale fish and lowered them to the shallow, rocky bottom. Starting the outboard motor again, he turned away from the spit and toward the last four markers. These were just a few yards in from the red, mournful bell buoy, which tolled the end of deep water. After they were tended, he could relax and make the mile-long trip across the bay to the dock, his work nearly done.

The thefts were mostly an irritation and made little sense. Not enough was involved to make selling worth

while, and as cheap as lobsters were in Podquit, it seemed
unlikely that anyone would go to all that trouble just to
eat them. Certainly he and old William Potter had lost
little. Indeed, they probably would not have noticed the
loss had the thefts occurred at random in the bed. But
if it was foolish always to strike in the same spot, there
was an element of safety in being that close to the
light and spit's end. This and a fast boat had kept Kip
from getting close enough to identify him. And when
he followed around to the sea, man and boat ceased to
exist. There was the real mystery . . .

He did not dwell on what had become an old story;
there was nothing new to be found in it today. Kip
hauled in the last pot. The lobster it held was three
or four years old and weighed less than a pound; it
needed another year or so to be big enough for eating.
He let it go home again, baited and lowered the pot,
and then stood to stretch his long legs and back for a
moment, tossed dark hair out of the way, and squinted
with sky-colored eyes at the southern horizon.

Two days before, in that far and warmer sea east of
the Lesser Antilles, the season's first hurricane had formed.
Her name was Anne, and she was reported as being a
small, intense storm moving slowly to the northeast.
Today, she had reached a position opposite Antigua in
the Leeward Islands.

The sky here could not hold Anne's threat; over South
Point, where fog had yet to encroach, it was blue made
brighter by white, darting gulls. But men who lived on
the sea and its shores, who were raised to the sound
and spirit, knew not to dismiss its whims or those violent

things born in its reaches. Peace and distance were never reasons for not wondering.

Something brought him back. Kip forgot that faraway wind, listened once more to water slapping against the dory, lobsters rustling in the basket, and the buoy's sad voice. Looking at the salt-burned bell, he had the odd feeling that he had heard it change—ring out of time with the waves. But the warmth of labor was gone from his body, and his clothes were wet from fathoms of dripping line; he shivered with new awareness of fog, and dismissed the small perplexity. It was time to go back.

The lobsters had to be put in the live-tank on the dock, and then he would go to Potter's cottage, just a few steps from the end of the dock. He would tell the old man about the day's catch. Potter, as usual, would pour cups of bitter tea, and if he was lonely, reach back into sea-years for a story; talk of sails, midnight sun, or China Sea, and of time gone and a younger man. And perhaps not remember that he had told it before.

Kip reached to start the motor, and before he could grasp and yank the lanyard, the dory moved and slowly turned. It was as if the boat had reacted to wind or some small, eddying current. But there was no wind—just drifting fog. And if a current, then, like that half-remembered change in a bell's ringing, it did not belong.

He sat still, wondering what had happened. There was no way of being certain about the bell; his mind had been on Anne. Too, although it had happened only seconds before, he could not recall exactly how the boat's turning had felt; it had been too subtle.

After two or three minutes, just as he was beginning

to feel foolish, that gentle surge came again, and the dory moved to an unseen force. This time, the boat followed a straight line. But this was the only difference, and as before, it soon stopped and left him without an explanation.

Curiosity gave way to an uneasiness that grew too easily among drifting patches of mist. Kip started the motor, and hurrying away from the edges of fog, pointed the bow for home.

Potter was not there when Kip reached the cottage. But he went in and put the kettle on the two-burner electric stove. Getting out the battered tin cups, he sat down to wait.

That small-windowed cottage was as old as America. Salt and time had turned its wood silver gray, and its thick pine floor was hollowed from countless footsteps. The roof was tight, though, and the walls solid; a place made for weather. And Potter kept it shipshape, "in Bristol fashion."

But it was resentful compromise, every bit of it—this place and the lobstering they shared. Potter had gone to sea when he was twelve, a stowaway on a Swedish merchantman, and went on to love and dare it for fifty years. Now he was seventy and not always graceful about it. Boats were not ships, and bays not the sea but home for conniving gulls; yes, and shallow refuge for those smart enough to leave a young man's game but who could not leave farther than the shore. How he roared when time made him restless! But it was better than nothing. Between lobstering and a pension, the old man had a living, and at least the sea *began* there.

He needed help, of course. Sometimes the weather got into his bones and kept him ashore. Kip recalled that day three summers before, when he'd been hired—Potter saying that a boy of thirteen with a widowed mother ought to be earning money "to ease that poor woman's burden." Potter started him off with 25% of what little they made, and soon betrayed himself by upping it to 50%, saying that a boy ought to be thinking of college, too. That was the way of this man who had roamed too long to have a family of his own.

Kip looked around at all that had grown familiar—thought again how nearly like a father the man had become. It was annoying at first, Potter jumping him as much as his mother did when, instead of studying, he spent too much time playing football behind Danver's drugstore or thinking about a girl, or when he wanted to spend some of his college money on an old convertible. But then he realized that now and then he wanted and needed a grown man's way of seeing. Potter filled some of the space left by a man who was lost on a remote Korean hill . . .

The water began to boil just as the old man returned. William Potter was a short, rather slight man who walked with a mariner's rolling gait. His eyes were like an osprey's and his face as scored by time and elements as any sea-jutting rock. But size was a lie, and age meant little; at seventy, his slender hands and arms were still made of ropes and cables, and his mind was laughter-quick. Some of that brightness smiled as he slid a box of canned goods onto the table and sat down.

Kip started the tea to steeping, and poured it when

it was dark enough. Taking his cup, the old man asked, "How was it today?"

"Pretty good. And our friend didn't pay a visit."

"Well." Potter noisily sipped the scalding brew. "One of these days we'll know who he is."

"Maybe," Kip said, thinking of the thief's talent for vanishing.

"You keep an eye. He's had blue water long enough now to feel pretty safe. And there's nothing like it for making a man careless."

The tea warmed him, and his clothes were nearly dry; he looked at the clock, feeling drowsy. "I've got to go soon. Mom will be home from work. Anything new on the hurricane?"

"No. Running as predicted."

Kip emptied his cup and frowned. "There's something funny."

"If it's the latest of Artemus Peabody's bad jokes, I've just heard it."

"No, I mean out by the buoy."

"Funny?"

"The bell rang the wrong way, and then the dory moved—twice—like a gust of wind pushed it, only there wasn't any wind. What do you suppose it was?"

Potter stared at him for a moment. "See anything?"

"No."

The old man finally shrugged. "The sea's always had its ghosts, boy. Sooner or later a man runs up against them."

"You don't really mean that," Kip said, looking for mischief in Potter's eyes. "You're making it up."

"Am I?" Potter laughed, but it was not the kind of

laugh that came from being found out. "Go on now, and my best to your mother."

Kip left and walked through town and up the hill toward the fence where his mother's roses grew. Ghosts? But *something* was out there . . .

CHAPTER 2

By late morning, when Kip again went into the bay with the dory, the fog had burned off. Although something of wondering remained, yesterday's uneasiness was gone. Potter's ghosts, real or merely humor's invention, had no place in this time. The wind was much too alive, the sky too deep and clear, and both the bay and the sea beyond were a blue-green nearly painful to regard. Even the gulls seemed enchanted, inclined to play in that brilliant hour rather than go seaward to follow after the trawlers for what could be stolen.

Remembering winter, a day like this was never dismissed as commonplace; summer grew old. Neither warm nor cold, the air was charged with the clean smell of sea water and made even work a pleasure. But, too, it was good just to enjoy the privacy of the bay; the village of Podquit had changed.

The year before, he and Potter had walked west of town to gape at the electronics plant nearing completion. That mass of concrete and glass intruded on the years, and so did the small apartment complex and the individual houses growing in once-quiet fields. But more than that, Podquit's population of six hundred, at that time, had been destined to reach over eight hundred, with a good number of the newcomers living right in town, in houses that had been vacant for years, or at most, rented to tourists. And it stunned . . .

Empty houses—shadowed porches and windows, growing vines, and echoes all but lost—this had been the dead part of the tree, the quiet fact of Podquit's past. It had faded for a time, grown smaller. There had been wars, of course, and a depression. Too, most of its young people had stayed only long enough to play, and had sought fortune, married, and had their children elsewhere. A few had come in from other places, and people had died. But just as water falls and finds its own level, a balance had been reached. And though it was smaller, most of the people who were part of that balance loved what they had.

Those who were not content hailed it as progress and new life—this sudden influx of strangers and the factory that would make miniaturized circuitry for rockets and computers. Podquit, they shouted, had finally come into the space age, where it belonged.

He remembered turning to Potter and asking, "Why here?"

"If you have a growing business and need another plant, you go looking for cheaper land and lower taxes."

"Well, I wish they had gone somewhere else."

A gull broke from its soaring to hover noisily behind the dory. It was a thief and a pest, but it was also beautiful. Kip reached into the bait box and tossed a bit of fish into the air for the gull to catch. With odd abruptness, the dory swerved off course, and for a moment his wondering about yesterday came afresh. To look upward at kiting gulls, though, was like glancing at fast-moving clouds. Equilibrium could be disturbed by it, and he supposed he had fallen against the tiller. And the gull still begged.

"No more," he said to it. "You're fat enough!"

Ignored for a while, the bird would leave. And Kip saw in the distance, then, three sailboats that were like the gull—white and clean, graceful. Not for work, they were delicate and toylike, bright playthings that were part of the change.

He remembered Potter calling it inevitable, the intrusion of the plant on what had used to be. Podquit could not stay in the past forever. The roaring giant that was the whole nation to the south and west of them had never ceased to grow. Hills and miles could not stop a day from coming.

There were other plants in the area—a paper mill and a shoe factory. And Podquit's only other lobster bed, a big one reaching all the way around South Point, supplied a cannery a few miles down the coast—a fact that luckily kept it from being competition for the old man. Each of these industries had had a time for being new and representing change, and indeed they had helped Podquit find that balance between growing and fading. But at least strangers had not been brought in to do the work.

The clamoring gull gone, motor, wind, and water were the only sounds. Turning away from those white sails, he glanced back at the dock. It seemed peaceful enough and unchanged, but that was only the illusion of distance. Distance was like last winter in the way it obscured. During the bitter months, newcomer and villager alike had stayed close to home and fire; it had almost been possible to forget. Even in his school there'd been few new faces. Most of the plant workers were in their twenties and thirties, and their children went to grammar school. It had not been until spring that anyone had really felt the impact—seen how many strange faces there were in the streets and shops. With good weather, the mooring space around the dock had grown crowded with fancy motorboats, and it had no longer seemed possible to repair pots or cut bait without someone in a garish shirt and sandals clicking a camera at him.

It was funny—what people were and what they only seemed to be. And it was not just the newcomers. Mayor Jack Fedders, naturally, was one of those who wanted to change Podquit. Having looked for industry, he was partly responsible for the new plant. The mayor quietly bemoaned the plant's hiring few local people, but bragged about the money the others would spend in town. Fedders had a big way, a big voice, and more than modest ambitions toward the state legislature.

But Kip had seen Big Jack with Terrence Wilcox, the plant's president, on the latter's fifty-foot cruiser *Nereid*. Wilcox did not seem in any way special. He was short and balding, mild in manner; a good business- man who loved boats, belonged to the Coast Guard Auxiliary, and liked an occasional dockside party. Noth- ing about him, personally, suggested wealth or great power and influence. Kip knew this, having met the man a few days earlier at his home. Indeed, Wilcox had taken a liking to him, which explained why he had hailed the boy as he passed, wet and dirty from work, and asked him to join the party for a while.

"Never apologize for the marks of hard work," Wilcox had said, dismissing his appearance. "Somebody bring the boy a coke!"

That was the man's way. Nevertheless, while everyone else sat on the deck or otherwise relaxed in an informal atmosphere, there at the edge of it was Big Jack—pinched up in a tuxedo, rigidly attached to a deck chair, and looking exactly like a small boy at a girls' tea. Maybe Potter was right when he said that Fedders was a big frog only because the pond was small.

The dory hit something then. Kip looked back, expecting and even hoping to see waterlogged driftwood come tumbling up in his wake. But there was nothing, and the bay was far too deep here for sand shoals or hidden rocks to be considered as even a remote possibility. Potter's ghost . . .

Kip stopped the motor and waited while the dory went dead in the water. Whatever its name, he was determined to end the mystery.

A few minutes passed without incident, and then, just as it had done yesterday, the boat slowly turned beneath him. It moved without visible explanation or sound, and stopped again.

With the passing of a good ten minutes, he did not know whether to be relieved or more upset. It was somewhat reassuring to drift undisturbed for that long; maybe the prankish sea spirit or whatever it was had tired of its game and was gone. But neither did he like being nagged by unanswered questions. Not only would it have been nice to know the cause; there was also the matter of how he was supposed to react. Could he go on about his work, or should he be hightailing it for the dock?

Kip reached for the starter cord without having made a decision, but to go on drifting seemed pointless. And perhaps it was wise to keep the motor going.

The motor failed to catch with the first yank of the lanyard, and before he could try again, he saw a shadow astern—the slightest darkening of the water, which, just short of the boat, shifted to white. It struck the dory gently, and then, some fifty feet away, a large triangular fin broke the surface.

Kip's first thought was of a huge shark, but when the whole broad back came surging out of the water, when he saw the shiny blackness of it, its almost bullet-shaped head and the graceful flukes, he realized that it was not a shark but one of the smaller species of whale. Yes, and quite capable of destroying or turning the dory over. Now his ghost had a name, and alarmed by it, Kip hastily got the motor going. He turned and sped for the safety of the dock.

Potter was there, waiting by the live-tank, where he had just finished selling lobsters to a few of the new people; he had seen Kip coming, and anger was in his face.

"What do you mean, running that old motor so hard! Are you trying to burn it up? And why are you back so soon when you've work to do?"

"If you'll give me a chance . . ." Kip sucked air into his lungs and leaned against the tank, shaking. "I ran into trouble. That ghost of yours . . ."

"Ghost? Oh . . . well, what about it?"

"It's a whale! A small whale, and it was pushing the dory around again! What are we going to do?"

The old man began to smile. "What kind? Did you get a look at it, or were you too busy inventing the first flying dory?"

"About fifteen feet long," Kip told him. "Round head,

like a bullet. Shiny black, white belly . . . and I think it had patches of white behind its eyes."

Potter nodded. "Killer whale. Half grown, I'd say, and weighing maybe three tons."

"Killer . . ." Kip felt a chill shoot through his stomach.

"Back off on that, boy. The name's misleading. A whale is as gentle a beast as you'll find in this world, sea or land. The killer is no exception."

"But he was pushing the dory, bumping against it, and . . ."

"Now the thing about whales is curiosity. The small ones anyway. Curious and playful. If I remember right, killers belong to the dolphin family. Clowns, boy. The biggest bunch of good-time Charlies you ever saw."

Kip digested all this and took a deep breath. "It's all right, then? To go back to work?"

"That's what I've been saying. But listen . . . if I were you, I'd keep a cable's length between me and that old pelican sitting on the boat next to ours. He's got his eyes closed, but he isn't asleep, and he's about as friendly as a Shanghai jailer." The old man squinted, and then added, "With a toothache . . ."

Reddening with Potter's teasing, Kip went back to the dory and out into the bay again.

He was still uneasy. There was little about the sea that the old man did not know, and what he said could be trusted. But three tons of curiosity was something to think about. The dory, after all, was not the Queen Mary.

With the whale very much on his mind, Kip reached the lobster bed and went to work. He saw it twice again during the afternoon, but only as a fin in the near distance.

CHAPTER 3

He had left his bed early and gone down to the dock when the bay ran red with the rising sun. It was not to work but to sit for a while and watch; to shiver with cold and the feeling of expectation that had awakened him. As if the bay would be different.

He had dreamed of whales, great schools of them, dark and spouting, coming in past Nancy's Light until there was not room left to wet a keel. And beyond the light, Anne's black wind had set the sea to boiling.

The dream, Kip supposed, came from going down to the library the evening before and reading what the encyclopedia had to say about whales. It was not a matter of doubting the old man; living and working at the edge of the sea, Kip had always been interested in its creatures. Curiosity had demanded that he also see it in print and perhaps learn more. The section on killer whales, or *Orcinus orca,* was small; apparently little was known about them. But Potter was right. They were the largest of dolphins, found in all oceans, and they traveled in pods of thirty or forty. The name "killer" seemed to come from the fact that they were the only kind known always to feed on other whales, seals, porpoises—the warm-blooded animals of the sea. And their manner of going about it was fearful. In sharklike bands, killers would surround a school of porpoises, each taking a turn at leaving the circle to attack and feed on the trapped animals . . . the sea running red from wholesale carnage. And though small, they had been known to attack even the blue whale, the largest animal in the world; tearing at its mouth and fins, and then retreating until the giant bled to death.

It was hard to equate that fierce creature with this playful character that had come to Podquit Bay, and with the old man's warm and assuring way of talking about it. But according to the book, there was no known instance of a killer ever having harmed a man.

As for the hurricane, he had listened to the news before going to bed. Expectations were that this day would find the storm as far north as Palm Beach and the Grand Bahamas, but well to the east. For the moment, Bermuda was the only land area threatened. But Anne had yet to swerve from her northward course, and it was this thought that had followed him into sleep.

It was foolish to be compelled by no more than a dream, to go out and look at his world to be sure it was as he had left it, and he knew this before he even left the house. But dreams that seem real could give taste to a morning, and at least it could be said that there was a whale in Podquit Bay. However, when the sun climbed and broke the mood, and he had gone out with the dory and worked through the lobster bed, even this became doubtful. He watched, but saw no sign of the whale.

Very likely it had returned to the sea, and Kip was not at all sorry at the thought. He could look back on yesterday's encounter as an interesting experience, but for all that, it still had been disconcerting to be an object of curiosity to a three-ton whale.

Then, as he finished with the last pot, realized that he had neglected to eat breakfast, and hurried back toward the dock, the bay's odd visitor was suddenly very much in evidence again. The whale's large fin sliced through the water close in front of the dory, and Kip had to swerve to avoid a collision.

"You crazy . . ." he yelled, and continued on his way, only to be forced, a moment later, to turn sharply again. Caution demanded that he slow down, but when he did, the whole boat was lifted part way out of the water. And before he could recover from that, the whale's flukes came slapping down to drench him thoroughly and leave an inch of water in the bottom of the dory.

It was enough to make him angry and enough to frighten him, and he did not know which to be or what to do. The whale stopped to watch him with oddly human eyes, made a strange whistling sound, and rolled over on its back almost coyly before beginning gracefully to circle the boat. There seemed, now, to be no malice, no threat in its motions. He remembered that Potter had talked of clowns, and realized then that the whale was playing, and that the drenching slap of the tail was invitation, the accident of exuberance, and perhaps even a sense of humor.

Kip sat there watching it happening, and wondered. It was real enough, and not at all an illusion. But, to him, it tasted of those preposterous things that dreams are made of—frog-prince fairy tales, and the Peaceable Kingdom, where all animals behave in unexpected ways. A *whale* playing with him?

The fact that it was a small whale helped some, but still thinking it was akin to associating with freight trains, Kip kept his eyes on the animal's circling, and very slowly continued in the direction of the dock.

Given this move to play with, the killer came out of its circling to touch the dory and then raced ahead to stop directly in the path of the boat. Steering to go around, Kip again found his way blocked and could not help beginning to grin at that oversized pest. Who ever heard of a three-ton kid, he thought. And yet it reminded him of one. Start, stop, start, stop . . . he could not move for more than a few yards without that creature rushing in like a spool-chasing kitten to bump the dory or stop in its way. Kip put up with it twice more, and suddenly broke the pattern by opening the throttle and speeding off in a different direction. Caught short by the unexpected change, the whale was now behind him.

"You aren't so smart!" Kip laughed and swung back on course.

What he had won was quickly lost; the lumbering old dory was no match for graceful, glistening speed. And that was how the game began; Kip no longer trying to escape, but just falling into it . . . an odd game of tag. Dock, home, the lobsters he had taken and the hour of the day . . . these things were forgotten in a bright time of spray and laughter.

When it was done, the whale was quiet in the water; floating on the surface as if tired. Kip brought the dory alongside and turned the motor off, still wondering. He knew that man and animals of many kinds had come together before without man having first to tame them.

If a creature had been given no reason to fear or distrust a man, then where was the miracle in their meeting? But to hear or read about such encounters and know the logic of it was one thing; what had happened in Podquit Bay was something else, though, and every inch a miracle, because this time it had happened to *him*. As if to confirm one sense with another, Kip reached out and touched the whale. It did not move from his hand, and this discovery completed the magic.

Reluctant to begin, Kip was now reluctant to leave. But after all that cavorting, the gas was low; this strange communion had to end if he was not to find himself rowing for the better part of a long and tide-running mile. When he moved away from its side, the whale slowly went somewhere deep . . .

"Go among them with harpoons and the will to harm, and whales are something to reckon with. But if paths merely cross, it's as if heaven were upside down . . . below instead of above, because they come like sea-angels and play. So happy and full of innocence . . . *innocence*. The sea is so big, Kip. I've heard it called the last free place on earth. I believe it, and I've wondered if elephants would not be like whales if they didn't have to share the land with us. But we crowd them, and kill them, and they have come to know us too well . . . more tea, boy?"

"No." Kip stirred from his dreaming. "I'd better get on home."

"I suppose. But listen," Potter said. "It's a nice thing that's happened to you. A privilege very few are lucky enough to know. But there are two things you've got to remember: The whale doesn't belong here. This isn't his world, and once his curiosity is satisfied he'll go on his way . . ."

"What do you mean, this isn't his world?" Kip interrupted. "Nothing the matter with this bay! You talk as though he was caught in a swimming pool!"

"No, it isn't the bay itself, although I doubt it'd support him when it comes to finding a square meal. I'm talking about being too close to people. It wouldn't surprise me if he wasn't gone already, but just in case he isn't, keep your mouth shut. Don't breathe a word to anyone. If it gets around that there's a whale in the bay, it'll start quite a fuss with those new people. You might even find some of them following you around in their boats. Understand?"

Kip nodded. "I won't say anything. Except maybe to mom."

"No! Not even to your mother! If she didn't have a heart attack, she'd skin me alive for letting you go out there!"

"I guess you're right."

"Okay . . . so let's get back to the first item. You've got to keep in mind the fact that it isn't going to last. You and that whale live in two different worlds. There couldn't be a greater difference if one of you had come from Mars. What you've got is only for the moment. All right?"

Kip left then and slowly walked toward home. Only for the moment? He could not believe such a thing. It had been too real and too good.

CHAPTER 4

On the fourth day, Kip moved away from the dock
and out into the bay more slowly than was usual. He
watched the water out there, the low line of the spit,
and was afraid of what might be true. The old man had
spoken of privilege, his being touched by the gay heart
of a black clown, and talked of that clown leaving.
Privilege . . . yesterday had grown in the night; he had
lived the brief encounter over and over again, and discovered it to be priceless. And because it was, maybe
he would be wrong in some way to ask or demand
anything and not just let it be.

Well, he wondered, why not let it be? Why put a
time to it? Kip did not see why, just because it was
some kind of gift, a privilege, there had to be an end to
it . . . at least so quickly. What did Potter know? The
old man had seen hundreds of whales in his day, of
course, but not this one and the way it had played.

Doubt began to fade, and he opened the throttle to
move at a pace more in keeping with that morning. The
brilliance of the air made the bay seem small. Halfway
out, he could still see a red paint can on the dock; its
color, no more than a pinpoint, leaped across the distance.
Such days became more frequent as summer moved
toward autumn. But, too, the hurricane had swerved to

the east, this morning, and Kip's awareness of that distant change made it part of the day and its colors.

He hurried on, certain now that all was well. And as if merely believing could make it so, the whale was there. Close to the sound of the red buoy, it lazed on the surface, spouting once, and perhaps enjoyed the sun's warmth.

The whale did not move as he drew near, did not show awareness of him even though its sensitive ears probably had detected the underwater pulsing of the dory's screw not long after he had left the dock. Only when Kip touched its glistening back did the whale stir and suddenly slip from sight. It surfaced again yards astern, made a graceful turn, and came straight for the boat.

Kip caught his breath and opened the throttle hard; laughing as the whale swerved at the last and raced alongside. They went fast for the open sea, coming about only when Nancy's Light was nearly astern. Although it could have done so with ease, the animal never pulled ahead, but kept pace with the boat in its swooping, almost birdlike way. Apparently it enjoyed the run much in the way a dog enjoyed running with a boy, following with enthusiasm every little turn. Kip went farther back along the spit than he had intended to go, and turned to keep the privacy of distance. And the whale made a game of the turn, its flukes rising and falling to send the water sheeting with a gunshot sound.

They had reached the buoy and were racing out into the bay when some small movement, a spark of color, caught Kip's attention—something not far from where he and the whale had turned around. With a chilling shock, he saw a man stand up on the spit and start walking back toward the dunes and the mainland. He slowed in the water, ending the game, and the whale went on and under, but the animal being out of sight now hardly made a difference. They must have come within a hundred yards of where that person had been sitting; he could not have missed seeing them.

Kip hesitated, not knowing what to do, but then turned and sped in that direction. His secret was out. But what could be done? What could he say? There was no way of making the whale a secret again, and, knowing this, he felt sick.

By the time he reached that part of the spit and pulled the dory onto the sand of a small beach there, the man had gone into the dunes and out of sight. Kip began to run, wondering which way he had gone. The spit was broad at that point, widening out to perhaps half a mile, but hummocks of sand and sea grass prevented him from seeing more than a short distance in any direction. He thought of fighting his way through steep, loose sand to the top of a hummock, but was afraid to stop running. It was not a matter of failing to find the man so much as it was the possible presence of other people in the dunes. Young men sometimes brought their girls to that windy solitude, and it was a good place for sun-bathing and picnics. Maybe there were people out there today, and maybe not, but the danger of it increased with every step taken toward the mainland. And all he could see in his mind was that man encountering some-one and pointing toward the bay, yelling, "Whale! There's a whale out there!" And then it would be as Potter had warned.

All he could do was run, his breath exploding, burning in his lungs. He found footprints to follow, but dry sand and wind had made them roundly ambiguous; they could have been hours old or new, leading toward the mainland or away from it.

Kip fought time, distance, and ebbing strength for another five long minutes before he stumbled, and crying out, fell in unexpected view of the man he had pursued. The latter turned, startled, and then came toward him.

"Is there something wrong? Are you all right?"

Kip did not have the breath to speak, but lay there staring at the man and realizing that it was someone he had seen before. Several times, earlier in the year, he had seen him on the spit, walking or looking out to sea. Somehow that tall figure, bent slightly in the wind, always suggested one who preferred being alone. But Kip had thought him to be an older man, and not one still in his forties. His hair, not matching a younger face, was pure silver.

"You must've been running pretty hard," the man said, helping him to sit up, and then almost pointing at him with sudden recognition. "You're the one out there . . . with the whale."

Kip nodded, gasping and feeling dizzy.

"My name is Harper. And you?"

"Kip . . ." he managed, almost strangling. "James . . ."

"I'm sorry. Don't try to talk," Harper cautioned, and then went on. "That's quite a playmate you have. A killer whale, if I'm not mistaken."

Again, Kip could only nod.

"The white markings . . ." Harper sat down beside

him. "I saw one in an oceanarium. But this is remarkable!"

Kip got to his knees, growing impatient with Harper's talking and his own inability to speak.

"Try taking deeper breaths," Harper suggested. "And relax. Remarkable . . . I suppose it's possible that the whale hasn't met humans before. What a blessed state . . ." He paused, and looking at Kip, seemed almost sad. "You can count on me to say nothing."

Kip succeeded in swallowing. "How . . . did you know?"

"What other reason would you have for running after me? Of course I understand! More than you do, perhaps." A kind of weariness crept into Harper's face.

"Potter, the man I work for, said there'd be people out here following me around in boats."

"Yes, and using the spit for a grandstand," Harper growled. "And it wouldn't be enough to look, and then let it be. Most might have good intentions, but few would realize that what works for you won't work for a crowd; by intruding, they unavoidably destroy. They'd keep at it until they drove the whale back out to sea."

"I'll just have to be more careful about playing with the whale, that's all."

Harper sighed. "I wish it were as easy as that."

"Well, isn't it? What else is there?"

"Kip, you and that whale are an anachronism. By that I mean, the two of you are out of step with the world around you. It's almost inevitable that something will happen. The whale can't remain a secret. Not for long. Look at me; on the spur of the moment, I go for a walk, and what happens? I see a boy and a whale racing in the bay! If nothing else, how do you hide a whale? How do you make him submerge if you see somebody coming?"

Kip could not argue with it. The man was right.

Abruptly, Harper stood up and climbed one of those hills of sand; sat in sea grass and looked at the bay. Kip found himself following.

"It *is* isolated out here. That's why I like it so much. Sometimes I have to get away from electronics and people . . . it isn't just being tired, and going home and shutting my door isn't always enough. The doorbell has a chime, and the phone persists. Here . . . rocks, sand, and wind. A privacy of spirit. Maybe privacy enough for a boy and a whale. I could be wrong in what I said, Kip."

"You mean I might be lucky."

"Yes."

Kip shrugged, and muttered, "Thanks a lot!"

Harper grinned at him. "I know. Well, for whatever it's worth, it's better to see something coming than to be caught short by it. And until something happens, take what you've got and make the most of it. Make sense?"

"I guess so."

"Good." Harper glanced at his watch and stood up. "Time for me to go. It's a long walk back."

"I can take you in the dory." Kip stirred from his thoughts.

"Thank you, but no. I need the exercise."

Kip watched him stiff-leg it down that spilling, shifting slope of sand and walk quietly away. Alone again, he sat there for a while staring at the bay but not really seeing it.

CHAPTER 5

Sleep did not diminish Harper's words or the way Potter, when told of the encounter, grunted and said the man probably was right. Morning held an anxiety that had Kip out of the house earlier than usual. He would have been earlier still, skipping breakfast, but his mother had heard him and came into the front room with wondering concern in her face.

"Sun's not even up yet." She made him close the door. "What's going on?"

"Nothing. I was awake and didn't want to stay in bed."

"Since when?" Christine yawned, tying her robe. "And when did breakfast stop being important? If William Potter thinks . . ."

"He doesn't have anything to do with it," Kip told her, wishing she would give in to sleepiness and go back to bed.

"Well . . . you've got something on your mind. For a couple of days now. Fidgeting, or staring off into space, and not listening to what I say."

"Maybe it's a girl." Kip tried joshing her.

"At this hour? Not likely." She tried to put her dark hair in order with her fingers, and then sighed. "But whatever it is, you still have to eat. Get to the table."

Afterward, he ran most of the way to the dock, resent-ing the speed with which the sun seemed to climb.

Instead of aiming for the lobster bed, he took the dory along the shore line and followed the spit from its beginnings. He watched shallow coves and grass-crested dunes, and twice turned the motor off to listen for the voices of children, the squawk of portable radios, anything that might betray the presence of people out there. Halfway between mainland and light, he even beached the dory and scrambled up one of those higher ridges of sand to look and listen again. But he found only the whisper of sea grass in the wind.

It was this emptiness that began to argue with Harper's prophecy, and, in Kip's mind, made that spine of sand and rock less of a threat and more as he remembered it. As if to suggest that yesterday had been an error and out of joint, even capricious Anne had returned to a north-ward course.

Kip went back to the dory, and on toward the bed. There had to be caution, he knew. As the man had said, Harper was his own best example of the danger. But having exercised a little care, he felt anxiety slipping away. Keeping the whale a secret no longer seemed to depend on luck; what had been described as inevitable now became merely possible. Maybe by using a little common sense, Kip thought, one made his own luck. There were never more than a few people in the dunes, and on most days, none at all. Rarely did anyone visit the light. But that aside, one reason the spit was empty now was the earliness of the hour. Why not limit his time with the whale, he asked himself, to the early mornings? Yes, and for added measure, it would be wise if he and

the whale stayed closer to the light or deeper in the
bay.

Again that sleek animal was near the red buoy as Kip
approached, and apparently asleep. He wondered if, like
cats, whales slept not when darkness came but when
they felt like it, and if his friend had not spent the night
hunting at sea.

Speeding up a little, Kip let out a whoop and cut
close enough to reach out and slap the animal on the
back. The killer slowly slipped out of sight with hardly
a ripple. Pulse pounding happily, and with that almost
nervous laughter of anticipation, he swung the boat hard
around the buoy and ran for the open bay. Somewhere
below, where light slanted and grew dim, the whale
would be keeping pace or charging ahead like a high-
balling freight train. Kip knew it, could see it in his
mind. But where would the hilarious ambush take place?
When and in what way? It was a game of tag in which
he could not keep from being "it" for very long. Soon . . .
any second now . . . in the growing suspense of it, he
held his breath and watched the water around him.
And waited . . .

But when the whale finally broke the surface, it was
well astern of the dory. Kip circled, still anticipating,
and then returned to the animal's side. For a moment,
it pushed the boat . . . and fell quiet once more, drifting.

Kip stroked its black hide, and wondered, "Hey pal,
what's the matter?"

The question fell on the air and had no meaning. He
wished for a language in common and not this difference
that muted and made them dumb. His hand was the
only link, and it could neither ask nor hear an answer.

For a while, the world was gone, and they drifted, belonging only to tide and wind. And it was enough; games were forgotten, shouting and laughter left for other moments. Only when the sharp cry of a close-skimming gull startled and made him look upward did Kip learn how far the sun had traveled.

"Maybe later we can play," he said. "But I've got work to do now."

He broke the water-quiet and the wind-quiet with the motor, and went back to the buoy and the bed. Reluctantly, and with a last glance at where the whale had been, he slipped into routine. Once it was begun, Kip soon ceased to quarrel with its demands of time. He worried a little about the whale, but then supposed that, like people, whales could not play the clown every day. And if not today, then perhaps tomorrow. He also thought about Anne. Holding to her northering way, she was now opposite the Carolinas . . . and was becoming more and more a matter of interest in Podquit. But again, what was true today might not be true tomorrow. The sky here still held no warnings, and far away, Anne could at any time put a hook in her course and die.

The whale was not to be seen when he was done. Kip had caught a quick glimpse of it near the rocks of the spit not far from Nancy's Light. But that had been nearly an hour ago, and he supposed the animal was somewhere deep in the bay or following curiosity to some other part of it. Or perhaps the whale had gone beyond the light to feed in the open sea. There was nothing to do but head for the dock and home; yes, and wait for tomorrow.

Lugging the basket toward the tank, Kip saw the Wilcox boy sitting on the deck of his father's big cruiser, and stopped. Running across Farley like that would usually have been worth a nod and nothing more. Although they had once started out to be, they were not friends. But Farley was pretending to be busy polishing the *Nereid*'s brightwork. It had to be pretense; the rag he was using was obviously a handkerchief whipped from his pocket, and the missing can of polish was as conspicuous as the wooden expression on his face. But given rag and polish, he still would have been suspect. Farley was not that ambitious.

Kip went on to dump the lobsters into the tank, wondering why his return from the bed should cause Farley to act that way? Why pretend to do anything? With the question, what Harper had said came to mind, and he stopped to look back at the *Nereid*. But then he relaxed; the boy was here, and not out there somewhere.

Farley had been an odd sort ever since he had come to Podquit last year. Maybe it was because he was one of the new people, and maybe, as Potter had said, he was only a spoiled rich kid.

They had met on the dock. Farley had been sent by his mother to buy some lobsters, and was amazed to find that the creatures he bought were alive. The humor of it seemed to embarrass him, and days passed before he returned and struck up a hesitant kind of conversation. Two or three weeks went by before Farley appeared again and invited him to his home. There, beyond the fact that Farley's room was cluttered with dozens of model airplanes, he learned little about the boy. Though eager to listen, Farley never said much, and this remained true the one time Kip took him out to the lobster bed. Clearly glad to be there, Farley still sat in the bow and not once began a conversation on his own.

Maybe it was simple shyness on Farley's part, but whatever the cause, Kip had never come to know him, really, and if time for growing accustomed was the answer, what happened soon thereafter left them without much chance for that.

Farley suddenly wanted to be a partner in working for the old man, and Kip had turned him down. The strange thing was that Farley asked in a way that was less a question than it was an assumption that, naturally, he would be hired. And when he said no, Kip remembered, it was as if the other had not even heard him.

"I know you'll have to teach me some of it, but I learn fast and I'll work hard . . ."

"Listen." Kip tried to stop him. "I told you we can't . . ."

"Dad says I'm lazy," Farley went on. "What they ask me to do at home . . . I could care, you know? But going out in a boat to bait traps and bring in lobsters, that's something else. And besides, it pays a salary. Allowances are for kids."

Almost too loudly, Kip said, "I told you *no.*"

"What?" Farley's mouth stayed open.

"There isn't enough money in it to pay three people. It's a small bed. Potter needs every penny he gets because his pension isn't enough, and I have to help my mother and save a little for college. We don't even need anyone. There isn't that much work."

Farley stared at him, and then turned to walk away. Beginning friendship ended there. From that day on,

Farley had barely acknowledged his existence, and Kip had not let himself be bothered by it.

But now Farley was behaving in an odd way, and not knowing why, Kip could not help being suspicious. He sat on the dock by the *Nereid* and looked down at the boy. Farley, like his father, had red hair and was short and rather pudgy. Pale and freckled, one of those who never tanned, all he had to show for summer was a raw, peeling nose.

After a long moment of being ignored, he said, "That's a good way to wear out a handkerchief."

Farley jumped a little, but replied without looking up, "I've got plenty."

"You ought to be using polish, too."

The other shrugged. "I don't know about that. A little spit and elbow grease works pretty good."

"Maybe," Kip told him. "I guess it's better than just sitting there."

"What do you mean by that?" Farley wanted to know. "Something wrong with sitting here? It's my dad's boat."

"No, nothing wrong." Kip began to wonder why it had seemed to matter. "I guess it hit me as being a little funny, you doing that."

Farley looked up at him for the first time, somewhat defensively, and said, "I suppose you don't think it's funny . . . what you've been doing out in the bay."

"What have I been doing?" Kip did not like the idea of having been watched, and again thought of Harper. Feeling the chill of possibility, he was cautious. "What's funny about lobstering?"

"Aw, come on, now." Farley gave him a sarcastic grin. "Since when do you have to zigzag and roar around like that to catch a lobster! I saw you. And you did it yesterday, too!"

Kip raised his eyes to reappraise a scene that had been his to look at almost every day of his life, and wondered if a whale could be seen that far away. The bell buoy was no more than a red speck, and the massive rocks of the spit were grains of sand. Nancy's Light was as big as a matchstick held at arm's length. The whale's fin and a glistening back rising a few inches above the surface were not likely to be seen, then, unless one knew the whale was there and knew exactly where to look. But what of those moments when with such exuberance the whale had leaped into air and sunlight?

"Oh, that . . ." Kip tried to dismiss it with a wave of his hand, and searched for an excuse.

"Yeah, *that.*"

"Just having some fun with the boat. You know how it is. Gets a little dull going straight out and straight back." It sounded reasonable, and for good measure he added, "I'd rather the old man didn't know."

Farley apparently accepted the explanation, and indeed seemed disappointed. Without another word, he came up the ladder to where Kip was sitting and walked away.

Kip sat there for a little while longer, relieved that the secret of the whale was still his. Farley did not know the meaning of what he had witnessed; certainly he would not have stopped the argument if he had seen something more than the boat. But what if curiosity persisted and he continued to watch? Harper had used the word *inevitable* . . .

CHAPTER 6

From the front window of Christine James's parlor, one saw roses, the roofs of town, and houses on an opposite hill, but not Podquit Bay. Kip stood by the glass watching evening come as if spit, light, and the sea beyond were part of the view. The day was done, supper over; it was at this time that he usually settled down to read or watch the television programs that came in over the cable. But this evening he could only stand or move restlessly about the room.

When his mother took the last dish into the kitchen and came out again, Kip gave in to it and said, "I think I'll go for a walk, Mom."

She hesitated, but then sat down and reached for the newspaper. "Where are you going?"

"I don't know. Maybe to Potter's for a minute."

"Seems to me you just came from there."

"Yes." He jammed his hands into his pockets, knowing that she was not really reading the paper. "Well, maybe I'll sit on the dock for a while and watch the bay. I don't know."

Her eyes left the paper and found the window. "I wish I knew what it was. There's something you're not saying, holding back. And it must be important. You seem worried, almost scared sometimes, and maybe if I knew what it was I could . . ."

"It's nothing, Mom. Just restless, that's all."

"Nothing?" She watched him with gentle exasperation, and said, "It's the nothings of a boy that cause gray hair!"

Halfway to the door, he turned and tried to imagine her with gray hair, but she was still young and too much like the roses she grew.

"Kip, I know there are private places in a boy, places where even I don't belong. But if something becomes too much to handle, then I have to know. All right?"

Kip nodded and tried to smile. He went out and through the gate between the roses, and watched the bay as he walked down the hill. It would have been difficult to give a name to exactly what was bothering him. He was not especially worried about the episode with Farley Wilcox; what was done was done and it found his secret still intact. But if Farley's curiosity had not been satisfied, it represented a possible difference, a change.

Neither was he concerned about the whale. It had not played as before, but perhaps it was tired, and again it seemed quite reasonable to assume that whales did not *always* feel like playing. He had been warned that it was not in the nature of such things to last; what he and the whale knew together had to end. To Kip, that made about as much sense as saying it could not begin. In the past, had anyone suggested he would play games with a whale, he would have scoffed and wondered at the other's wild imagination. But it *had* happened, and if that was not a miracle neither was its continuing.

Still, there they were . . . small changes. Farley had

seen half of the game and grown curious, and the whale's
exuberance was less than yesterday. Harper had talked
of inevitability, and in another way, so had Potter. These
things combined to nag and lend uneasiness to the hour.
It was like that storm down-Atlantic. Hundreds of miles
away, it was not a threat. How many hurricanes ever
came that far north? But in the roar of distant gales
there was always a whisper that said *maybe* . . .

Reaching the waterfront, Kip went on past Potter's
and out on the dock to stand and stare at Nancy's Light.
The sun had not been down for long, and the bay was
a place of dark water and the beginnings of fog. There
was a little time left, if he did not waste it.

Climbing down to the dory and starting its motor, he
quickly moved out into that world of blue and shifting
patches of gray. Kip did not know where the whale
might be or that he would even find the animal before
it became too dark to see. But he felt better looking,
doing something.

The first place he aimed for, of course, was the lobster
bed. Not once since the whale had arrived had he found
it far from there. Perhaps it liked the red buoy's bell.

Rather than risk ramming the whale, who might be
sleeping on the surface, Kip slowed down when he was
perhaps a hundred fifty yards out from the bed . . .
and was startled by the sound of another motor coughing
into life. He stiffened at the tiller and strained to stare
in the direction of the sound but could not see much of
anything in that murky light. The patches of mist were
heavier, here, and when he located the other boat, it
was the merest suggestion of one beginning to move

away. The figure hunched at its stern was hardly more than a shadow, but in veiled appearance he discovered a hint of familiar detail. Pale blue denims, dark-headed . . . as before.

He had never known any more than that, but Kip did not hesitate. It was the lobster thief. He opened the throttle and aimed the dory in an attempt to intercept him. But the other's boat was light and fast, and once again he knew the frustration of seeing it pull away. Now, as before, outright pursuit was futile; by the time he reached the spit, the thief had gained the light and was out of view.

It had always been this way; the fog or the darkness, or both, and the thief speeding around spit's end to escape into the edges of the open sea. But suspecting that the interval between them had been shorter this time, Kip beached the dory among the rocks and scrambled across the spit in hopes of catching a glimpse of the fugitive going by or hiding somewhere on that side.

Nancy's brooding finger pointed skyward, and wisps of mist sailed silently like an endless lost fleet of Flying Dutchmen, and the sea came to strike the rocks beneath him. Nothing else was there to be heard or seen. It was as if he had gone chasing after something no more substantial than one of Potter's sea ghosts. Kip could not believe in such a thing, and he tried to argue with it. The whale had proved a point, hadn't it? The unknown had appeared, and regardless of the old man's suggestion, made seriously or not, was anything but supernatural. But this man and boat . . . here the *known*, the seemingly tangible, *vanished!*

As soon as the thief rounded the point, the sound of his motor always stopped. Knowing that much, it was reasonable to assume that he could be just a short distance away, drifting silently and using fog or darkness for cover. But never to see his boat reach the other side, not to hear its motor again or the creak of an oar no matter how long he waited and stayed out of sight . . . well, the thief apparently had the ability to stop existing. Ghost? In spite of himself, Kip was beginning to wonder if that were an explanation.

Why not, he thought, as he walked down to the base of the lighthouse. If one accepted legend, then ghosts had been here before. The light that had once burned here had first reached seaward at the beginning of the nineteenth century, and had been known then as Makem's Light. Makem's daughter was a dark-haired girl named Nancy, and according to legend she heard voices in storms when the sea was high and the light not as easily seen—heard the crying of lost seamen, their fists pounding against the outside wall. Some who told the story said that Makem thought her to be quite mad and had to bind her arms and feet whenever the wind began to grow. Others said that what she heard was real, and that she tried not to listen. But however it was, one night when the sea was raging white across the spit, Nancy Makem went out to find her voices . . .

Like many, the light had gone out of operation with the advent of radio beacons and radar. Abandoned and neglected, its old spiral stairway no longer safe, Nancy's Light had been locked for as long as he could remember. It was just an empty shell, then, but Kip shuddered with the chill of more than fog, and walked back toward his boat.

Passing near a tidal pool formed by surrounding rocks and a submerged part of the spit, he saw the last of dim light glinting on a shiny surface. He was sure it could not be the thief's boat, but he went to check on it anyway . . . and found the whale.

"What in the world," he whispered, "are you doing here?"

Kip could not be certain that the whale did not spend every night here. Maybe it liked sleeping in that quieter water, but it still seemed strange and somehow connected with the animal's behavior earlier that day. He sat there for a while, watching and puzzling, but then the light was gone and he had to leave. Finding his boat again, and pushing away from the rocks, he let the town lights guide him back across the bay.

"Well, I don't think there's any doubt about it." Potter yawned and glanced wistfully toward his bed. "Your whale is sick. That's why he came here. Looking for snug harbor."

"But the way he was playing yesterday . . ."

"That doesn't have to mean anything," the old man told him. "Who can say? Maybe they can sense these things coming, and might be it was slow to wear him down."

It seemed reasonable to Kip, and he asked, "What do I do now?"

"Give him an aspirin and stick a thermometer in his mouth."

"That isn't funny!" Kip frowned at him.

"Okay, so it isn't funny." Potter snorted. "But just what do you think can be done?"

"I don't know . . ."

"Well, heave to and think about it. What the whale has done for himself is the best that can be done. He's found himself quiet water where he can be sick without his enemies taking advantage of it. Time tells the rest. He will get well or he will die."

"Die!" Kip jumped up from his chair, completely unprepared for such a notion.

Potter waved him back. "Just hold off and quit digging crabs! It *could* die. *Maybe.* I don't know what's the matter with it and neither do you. But it's a young whale, Kip, and that counts for a lot. I think other people finding it is probably your biggest worry."

Kip shrugged. "I suppose. But the way things are now, I'm not so sure."

"Why? Because you're not chasing each other all over the bay? Could be. And I'll admit the spit isn't like Main Street. But that's no guarantee. It *could* happen. Easily. If nothing else, every time our pots are robbed there is someone very close to the whale. He was out there this evening and not far from those rocks when you chased him."

Kip stared at Potter for a moment and then clutched his knees quietly. "It was getting dark, and the rain made it even harder to see anything. You're right, though. The rain won't last, and he'll be back. And other people . . . I know it's possible, but I keep hoping . . ."

"Go on home and get some sleep." Potter's gruffness was gone. "You'll have to wait and see if anything happens before you can know what to do. Go on! I'd like to get some shut-eye myself. Been feeling a little poor, lately."

"I'm sorry."

"Don't be sorry. Just relax and see where the wind takes you."

CHAPTER 7

Walking down the hill from his mother's house and through the streets of town, Kip was too tired really to acknowledge the fact of a new morning or the work that awaited him. He had slept little. Night had been made long and restless by too much worrying about the whale. Yes, and when sleep finally did come, it was given to endless pursuit of a phantom—a vaporous boat and a man made of mist who smiled and scattered in the wind whenever Kip came too near.

The fear that the whale might be dying had returned, been wrestled with and then pushed away. It remained a possibility, or the old man would not have mentioned it in the first place. But Potter had also spoken of the whale's being young, and Kip held on to this because he had seen its exuberance and known its joy, and because it was the only thing he could believe. As far as Kip was concerned, the whale's getting well was only a question of time. But its remaining undiscovered while it recuperated in the tidal pool . . . well, as Potter had said, there was no guarantee.

Nothing had changed out there. Those who visited the spit went to the dunes to picnic, or searched its nearer beaches at low tide for starfish. Apparently Nancy's Light was no longer a novelty among the newcomers; except for Harper, it had been months since he had seen anyone walk that distance to gape at the towering relic. And yet, who could say that it would not happen again today or tomorrow? At this moment, a car full of tourists from Kansas or Oklahoma might be stopping on the waterfront. And perhaps new to the shore and never having seen a lighthouse, one of them would suggest a long walk.

Kip had a way to lessen the chances of the lobster thief's spotting the whale, if Potter would agree to it. But, no matter how remote, this other thing nagged and he wanted to talk to the old man about it again and see if he had any ideas.

Potter was not at home when he got there, but Kip found him waiting by the dory. The old man grunted his approval and said, "I had an idea you'd be early, and it's a good thing . . ."

"Well, I wanted to talk about the whale . . . it being seen while it's in the pool. I was thinking of moving or bringing in the pots that are closest to the spit, if it's all right with you. Then our thief wouldn't be going as close to the whale. And I wondered if you had any ideas about the others, and . . ."

"You're wasting good wind, boy." Potter had a strange look in his face. "How do you figure it matters now?"

"What do you mean?" Kip did not understand. "Last night you said . . ."

The old man sighed impatiently. "That was last night. Kip, haven't you heard the radio this morning? It's Anne. She's off the New Jersey coast a couple of hundred miles. Picked up speed in the last twelve hours."

"She's going to hit here?"

"We'll know that by tomorrow, but she's close enough

to be an excuse for sweating, and we can't gamble with it. When you get them emptied, I want all the pots brought in. And before the day's over, we have to get the dory out and into the shed."

Kip nodded, and looked out toward the spit. "What happens to the whale?"

"What do you want me to say?" Potter's voice was quiet. "You've seen the spit when a storm's got the sea up. You better leave nature to itself and get on with what you have to do."

The possibility of Anne had been there all along, but his knees trembled a little when he went down the ladder to the dory.

Once into the bay, Kip realized how blind he had been. High cirrus clouds, like fine haze, had appeared in the southern sky; the sunlight here had a dead and brassy quality. But more obvious, the bay seemed made of glass, and the sea beyond came to the spit in long, rolling swells. Even the gulls seemed affected by the atmosphere. Their cries and wheeling spirits, which always seemed an essential part of wind and sea, were for the most part terribly absent. His world was not what it had been yesterday, and what was coming to it weighed heavily.

As for the whale, it was all very simple and very brutal. There had been no need for Potter to spell it out. The whale was part of the sea, and from it would know what was coming. If it had the strength to move, it would leave for the safety of the deeper sea . . . and the danger of falling victim to its enemies. If it had to stay, then it would perish when the hurricane struck and buried the spit with waves of unimaginable force.

There was work to be done, but Kip headed straight for that place among the rocks where the animal had taken refuge. Under the circumstances, he did not know what he wanted . . . to find the whale still there, or gone.

Fortunately or otherwise, it was still there and stirred only slightly at his touch. He sat with the whale for a few minutes, wordless and at a complete loss. There had to be an alternative somewhere, but he could not find it. With growing despair, he returned to his boat and tried to discover some comfort in labor.

The catch had to be put in the basket, and the pots loaded into the dory; they had not been brought in all at once since he went to work for Potter, but he guessed it would require at least two trips. Each pot with its marker buoy and a few fathoms of rope took up a fair amount of space. And then, as the old man had said, they would have to put the boat on the hoists and get it out of the water. After that, he still would not be done, because he had to go home and get everything ready— close the storm shutters, check the candle supply, fill a few jugs with water, and bring in wood for the fireplace. All too often, the power lines were carried away when high winds battered that coast. And for whatever time they were down, there was no electricity for the water pump, the stove, and the lights. The furnace burned oil, but depended on an electric motor.

Work did not keep worries at a distance. Kip kept butting up against the impossible, looking for solutions that did not exist. He wanted to move the whale away from what would be a fatal combination of rocks and pounding sea. How? He wanted the whale gone without its being prey to sharks, and where it would still have reason to come back when the storm was gone. Where? There was no answer to any of it. He could neither accept nor ignore the fact that he was up against an inalterable force of nature. Failing all else, if this was to be the last of their time, he would have liked to spend that day on the spit. But the preparations Anne made necessary deprived him even of that. And it was not fair . . .

When he reached the dock on the first trip back, Kip found Farley sitting on his father's cruiser with binoculars hanging around his neck. Loaded down with the basket, he would have gone on by, but Farley stopped him.

"No games today. What's the matter? Boat wearing out?"

"There's a hurricane coming, in case you didn't know," he said, and then with sarcasm, added, "If you can see past the end of that fancy putt-putt with those glasses, you might notice the sky looks a little funny."

Farley reddened and then, recovering, smiled. "I know about Anne coming. And for your information, wise guy, I can see pretty far with the binocs. Far enough to know you weren't just working out there. You had time for something else . . . like sitting on a rock, daydreaming."

Maybe such things did not matter any more, but he still found Farley's comment alarming and wondered just how much he had seen.

"I'll bet!" he said, as if sitting on a rock were not important. "With those little things? Why the old man's got a telescope that would do better than that with its dust caps on!"

"Oh yeah, well maybe you'd better take a look before you go shooting your mouth off any more! Here! Come down and look!"

It was exactly what Kip had hoped he would say, and he went aboard the *Nereid* quickly before the other could change his mind. He focused the glasses on the spit, and found the rocks forming the tidal pool. But it was not a close view, and in any case there was not the slightest hint of what the pool contained; the angle was wrong.

He handed the binoculars back to Farley, and shrugged. "Not bad," he said. "They're really pretty good—for binoculars."

Kip climbed back onto the dock and went on to the live-tank and to find the old man. Potter was in his cottage, listening to the radio.

"Still coming?" Kip asked.

"Like the angriest woman alive! You done out there?"

"No. I brought the catch in and a few of the pots. It needs another trip."

"Well, I'll come along and bear a hand. When we get back, we'll haul the whole thing out on the hoists and roll it into the shed all at once. Then we can hide and let her blow. You ready?"

"Yes," Kip replied, but held back. "You sound like you're catching cold."

"Been catching it for a week, now. Twisty-tailed bug! But a little salt air might do me some good."

Farley Wilcox was gone when they went to the dory, pulled those few pots up on the dock, and left.

Potter was quiet most of the way. It had been days since he had put on his old, yellow oilskin and gone away from land. The old man seemed most at home there, hunched over on the thwart and squinting seaward or toward the sky. He sniffed at the air now, and grinned back at Kip.

"Yes sir. Salt air is good. And when you get right down to it, so is a hurricane . . . for a younger man. I remember. Troubles hang to a man like barnacles, and when he gets rattled around by something walloping big . . . well, he comes out of it feeling all scraped down and proper again. Yes, I remember . . ."

CHAPTER 8

Kip stayed awake most of that night, waiting for the first eerie song of a rising and different wind. The stage was set for it with an unnatural quiet—that heavy, forbidding air. Even the stars, before they disappeared behind clouds, had seemed sullen and farther away. But the day had been demanding, he had slept little the night before, and his vigil came to an end without his ever knowing it.

Startled, he awoke at dawn to rain but not Anne . . .

He heard the story over the kitchen radio. Up and down the coast, people had been braced and ready for a bad blow. But hurricanes were unpredictable at best, and Anne was like all her violent sisters. In the small hours before dawn, she had turned northeastward and was now thought to be breaking up. And Podquit, as if caught in the shadow of her dark and gloomy gown, knew nothing worse than an echoed anger.

The tides were up. But the worst storm tides occurred in front of a hurricane and to the right of the center's line of travel, and so had missed them. Heavy, black clouds blotted out the light of beginning day and at erratic intervals unleashed a hard, drenching rain. Yet, to Kip, it was almost the very best of times. He had only the whale's sickness and the risk of discovery to consider.

Compared to what Anne could have done, it was a bearable alternative.

Old man Potter, he knew, would not want the pots returned to the lobster bed before tomorrow; it was not a day for working. But shortly after invisible sunrise, Kip went down to his cottage anyway, expecting at least to get the dory back into the water. He wanted, some time that day, to check on the whale.

Potter, being a practical sort and given to the mariner's habit of keeping everything shipshape, had different ideas.

"As long as we got the old tub out of the water," he said, "we might as well recalk some of its seams. And it's about time to paint its bottom, too . . ."

Kip began to grumble. "Can't all that wait? Cold weather will be coming soon, and the lobsters will move to deep water . . . why not do it then?"

"The painting can wait, come to think of it. It'll want time to dry properly. But with a whole day fit for nothing else, why not do some calking? Lately, she's been showing more water than working could make. You got something better to do?"

"Well," Kip admitted. "I wanted to go out to the spit and see how the whale's doing."

"I kind of thought that's what you were steering for." Potter gave him an exasperated grin. "But you might as well forget it. Tide's up, swells breaking the width of the spit, rain. Bad enough out there to have a dead cat running for a dry place! You couldn't stay, and I sure don't want your mom down here chewing chunks out of my backbone for letting you get pneumonia.

Besides, you know you can't do anything for the whale. It will die or get well whether you look at it or not."

The old man really didn't understand, Kip decided, and it was pointless to go on arguing with him. At best, all he could do was start the job and hope he did not find too much that had to be done. With any kind of luck at all, he might yet be able to use the dory that afternoon.

Kip went out to the shed, uncoiled and plugged in a long work light, and found those seams that were most obvious in their disrepair. They had to be stripped, first. Then, with a chisel-like calking iron, yarn of oakum had to be driven in. When that was done, melted pitch had to be paid along the seam. It could not be hurried, and it could not be a half-baked job. The old man was particular, and for that matter so was he, but with the worst of it done, Potter might be willing to let the rest wait until cold weather.

He worked at it for the better part of an hour and then went to stand in the doorway to watch the water and work the cramp out of his fingers. Except for areas of light drizzle, the rain had stopped for a while. The spit was a thin, murky line of stone, and the spray that burst across it at intervals from the seaward side looked, from that distance, like the smoke of an artillery barrage. And there in the northern curve of the bay, a small boat had begun to follow the spit out toward Nancy's Light . . .

Ignoring his own wish to be out there, Kip could not help wondering what reason anyone would have for taking a boat into the bay in that kind of weather. It did not make sense. His first thought was that friend thief was out to raid the lobster bed again. Since all the pots had been brought in, this seemed highly unlikely . . . unless, of course, the man did not know that much about lobstering. But even if the pots had been out there, he could not imagine anyone wanting a few lobsters badly enough to go after them this day. More likely, though just as silly, one of the newcomers in town was feeling adventurous . . . maybe a camera bug wanting a picture of the lighthouse with spray kicking up.

For all his rationalizing, it was still hard to accept. But there it was, the physical fact of a boat. Kip did not hesitate for long. No matter who it was or why, he was afraid the whale might be discovered.

He did not give the old man a chance to argue about it, but stopped in the doorway just long enough to say, "If you see Artemus Peabody, tell him I've borrowed his boat! Explain later!"

Kip sprinted down to the small, rocky beach that reached away on either side of where the dock began. The few boats that had not been taken away were overturned and lashed to stakes fifty feet or so from water's edge. It was not much protection against a hurricane, but some of the boats belonged to people who did not have trailers, or like Peabody, who lived over his own grocery, did not have a yard or a garage. He chose Peabody's because it was one of those small, stubby aluminum jobs and would be easy enough for one person to move down to the water. There was no time to go looking for help. Too, it was a fast boat, maybe faster than the thief's . . . if that was who it was out there.

He had just started the motor and zipped past the

end of the dock when that hard rain began again. The sudden drop in visibility did not bother him; he could estimate the position of the other boat. And the rain would prevent its occupant from seeing him coming.

When he was near the center of the bay, Kip no longer relied on the drumming of the rain to mask the sound of his motor but cut his speed down to a crawl.

A few minutes later, when he could hear the bell buoy and the sound of the sea beating against the spit, he turned the motor off and drifted . . . waited quietly in the rain.

CHAPTER 9

Once again the dark and obscuring rain subsided, fell
away to a thin gauze of drizzle and shifting mists. Seen
through it, the near bay and that dim line of embattled
granite was not quite real but more like a faded etching
held too close to the eyes.

For what seemed a long time, Kip heard only the
gradual approach of a motor—a sound often lost in the
boom and hiss of breaking sea. But then the other boat
came into view, so vaguely as to seem no more than
a darkening of smoke. Realizing that he had been too
cautious and ought to be closer, he reached for the
starter cord . . . but resisted the temptation. On second
thought, there did not appear to be much chance of that
person's accidentally spotting the whale from his boat;
he was keeping healthy yards between rocks and hull.
And Kip did not want to call attention to himself and
the curious fact of having been waiting there with motor
off, unless it was absolutely necessary to create a diver-
sion. That necessity would most likely arise only if the
man had it in mind to go ashore and walk to the light.

Normally, it probably would not have mattered. But
with the water as high and rough as it was, the usual
practice of tying a boat to a rock was out of the question.
Today, one would have to pull it out on the sand above

one of the little beaches. And the last of those beaches, that far out on the spit, was only yards from the whale.

"Just keep on going, mister," Kip whispered. He supposed that the best thing, if he had to intervene, was to claim a motor breakdown and ask to be towed back to the dock.

The other reached the lobster bed then, crossed its length, and faded out of sight. Relieved, Kip took a deep breath. Apparently it was nothing more than someone out for a boat ride. It took all kinds, he guessed, and this one obviously got a kick out of cruising around in rough water.

But he had no sooner made this appraisal than the boat reappeared in the bed . . . and stopped. A moment later, it turned away from the spit and moved slowly in the general direction of the bell buoy, as if its position, in that obscuring drizzle, was less than certain. Kip watched as the boat came closer, wondering if he ought to stay put or get away from there; he had not counted on something like this. As the distance grew less, he could see more clearly . . . and suddenly realized that the man was dark-headed and wore pale blue denims. At nearly the same moment, that shadowy figure spotted him, stiffened, and went roaring out of sight.

In an instant, Kip was speeding after him. He opened the throttle wide in hard pursuit down toward the light, and soon closed it again. All that extra power, he discovered, was almost pointless when he could not see or even hear the other boat; the thief had only to stop just out of sight somewhere and let him go zipping by like an idiot. More than that, Kip had no intention of taking the little teacup of a boat around the point. Both bay and sea reacted to the strong influence of Anne, but the spit was stopping the worst of it.

Just short of the light, then, Kip killed the motor and listened . . . and heard only the sea. It was too discouraging. To believe that, for once, he had all the advantage and *still* lost the game . . . it was just too much. Wet and feeling chilled, he gave it up and started back.

Knowing that there might not be another chance that day, he wanted at least to check on his friend while he was there. Kip moved along the spit until he reached that small beach just beyond the whale. The beach itself was under water, of course. But the spit was less abrupt there, a slope of sand and pebbles reaching away to where hardy clumps of dune grass grew. Kip nosed into it and jumped out to pull the boat away from surging water. It would be safe there.

For an instant, when he reached the tidal pool, Kip thought that the whale was gone. But then the water went foaming out through the rocks to reveal the animal's broad, shining back.

He sat down and watched for a few minutes. This visit, though, was even more frustrating than the last. It was bad enough, before, to sit in silence and have nothing left of what had been a joyous game. But at least it had been peaceful. Now, the day was touched by distant anger, full of gloom, and cold fragments of sea came hissing over the spit to drench him. And except for brief intervals, he could not see his friend. The best that could be said of it was that the whale was still alive, and, if outward appearance meant anything at all, seemed to be holding its own.

Kip had to be satisfied with that, and got up to leave. He needed a mug of hot tea and to dry his clothes on the old man's stove, and he had work to do if the dory was to be ready tomorrow. But something about the thief and his way of disappearing had stuck in his mind as more than a mere annoyance. It was crazy, to find himself staring at Nancy's Light and actually wondering if it might hold the answer. How? Neglected and no longer safe inside, it had been locked up for at least twenty years. And that part of it aside, where was the boat? Folded up in the thief's back pocket? Hardly. Still he could not leave the notion alone, and began walking down toward that ominous, mist-shrouded tower. Halfway up, on the landward side, it had a window— a black socket in bone that still saw as if an eye remained— and he watched it, growing more and more uncomfortable as he went.

The whole thing was getting sillier and sillier, he told himself, and that old, massive door with its huge hinges convinced him that he should stop wasting time and go home. The latch and hinges were so heavily corroded by salt that he doubted that the door would open even if it were unlocked. But on the latch side, there was a little space between frame and door's edge that he had not noticed before.

Probably the building had settled that way, Kip thought, or the door had warped for lack of paint. Just so there would not be any question about it to nag him later, he pushed against it . . . and the door moved. Hardly believing it, he put his shoulder to it and pushed again, and the door was open. It sagged and protested, but apparently it was this condition that had kept the door

closed against the wind; the latch had ceased to function
long before.

Common sense told him that he ought to go home and
get a flashlight before messing around with that place
and whatever was in there. But he chided himself for
worrying about something or someone's being inside. It
was too logical—no boat, no man. All considered, then,
the only question left was, why go in at all? Kip did
not have the answer to that, or why the lighthouse
continued to nag. As if the dark could rob him of it,
he held his breath and went in.

A few steps beyond the door, he stopped and waited
for his eyes to adapt. Light came from behind him, of
course, and there were two windows above. Beyond
them, at the very top, where the old reflectors used to
turn, there was more light coming in. But even after he
was ready, it was not enough—not on that gloomy day.
He could see degrees of shadow—masses but not detail.
And he could move, but only by feeling his way. The
big problem was that the upper part of the stairway
had collapsed and fallen sometime in the past. Its wreck-
age made a puzzle of the floor.

Again he wondered why he persisted. Kip felt no
particular curiosity about the place. There had been times
when he had wished he could have gone to the top,
as if one could see more from there than from the higher
hills. But now it was a ruin, and he was limited to its
floor. Why stay? Below the echoing sound of the sea,
something about it whispered to him. He searched for
anything that might burn and make a light.

Kip found the remains of a cardboard carton. It was
a little damp, but he supposed this might let it burn

longer. The big question, after he had been soaked to the skin, was whether or not his matches had survived. He pulled the box out of his pocket and was dismayed to find most of them stuck together and useless. But he found one down in the center that worked, and got his cardboard going.

It was not much help; by holding it up he could just see well enough to pick his way slowly around the debris and toward the opposite wall.

But when he came close to the stairway, a shadow moved and made a sound.

Kip thrust the light higher over his head, trying to see, and called out, "Who's there?"

Answered by silence, he wondered if there might be rats living there. Going closer, he tested the first step with his weight, and then the second . . . and from there, he could just see the dim shape of someone huddled on the stairs above him. The flame reached his fingers then, and he had to drop the cardboard before seeing the other's face.

Deciding to gamble, he said, "All right, I saw you! Might as well come down. The game's over."

"Get off my back!" the other yelled. "Go away!"

Kip knew the voice, and could not believe it. "Farley?"

"I'm warning you! Don't come any closer!"

Kip took another step up the staircase and stopped. The whole thing was becoming preposterous. The matter of the missing boat had yet to be solved, and he could not imagine Farley as the lobster thief, that phantom with the substance of smoke. Besides, Farley was a redhead and the thief had always appeared to him as dark-haired. It occurred to him then that Farley could have walked to the lighthouse and that his being there was only coincidental with the appearance of a boat along the spit. But why was he hiding in the dark, and acting as though he had been caught at something?

"I don't get it," he said, going closer, and suddenly Farley's fist came shooting out of the gloom to graze his cheek.

Immediately and instinctively, Kip swung at that vague shadow before him and caught Farley squarely in the eye. Crying out, the latter tried to come down but collided with Kip, and they began to grapple on the staircase.

He found Farley surprisingly strong but finally managed to pin him down. "Now . . ." he fought for breath. "You listen . . ."

"No . . ." Farley's voice broke with frustration. "Let go!"

"Not until you . . . answer questions!"

The Wilcox boy twisted hard and almost broke loose; flailing and kicking, he scrabbled backward up the stairs for a few steps before Kip tackled him. And with the impact, that shift in weight, something snapped, and the staircase seemed to twist—felt as if it were sagging and moving away from the wall. Both boys froze.

CHAPTER 10

"It's going to collapse . . ." Kip whispered hoarsely.

"We'll be killed!" Farley wailed, close to panic.

"Shut up!" Kip warned. "And don't be such a baby!"

"I'm no baby . . ."

"Then hold still and do as I say! Do you understand?"

"Okay . . ." Farley's voice was strained, tense, a wire close to snapping. But he had control of himself, now.

Kip took a deep breath. "All right . . . we're going to get off this thing, but we've got to do it a little at a time . . . and if it starts wobbling around too much, we stop until it stops . . . okay?"

"I guess so."

"Okay . . . the first thing I'm going to do is let go of your legs. When I do, don't move them. Don't move at all until I tell you. Maybe if we're a few feet apart and don't have our weight all in one place . . . maybe it will hold. You got me?"

"Yes . . ."

Kip gradually released his grip, and very slowly eased his way down until there were four or five steps between them. As careful as he was, the staircase swayed and shook.

He waited until it stopped, and then said, "All right, you can start now . . . but keep it slow and gentle, an inch at a time, and stay close to the wall as you come."

When he felt Farley beginning to move and was certain he was doing as he had been told, Kip started downward again. He did not know how far up they were. He had been too engrossed in finding out who was on the stairs to pay attention, and the fight had taken them higher. The position of the door from there would have told him, and so would the dim jumble of floor, but from that close to the wall he could see neither and did not dare move to look. He knew that it was not much, maybe ten or twelve feet, certainly no more than twenty . . . not a dizzying height. But it was far enough when it came to falling, and the worst of it was that the staircase would be pulling apart and falling with them.

Both that thought and the increased motion of the stairs made him stop, and he called out to Farley to do the same.

"Aw, come on, now!" Farley could barely speak. "This is too much . . . aren't we almost there?"

"Almost," he guessed, and when the swaying stopped, added, "But we still have to take it slow. All right. Come on."

The painful journey was resumed, each inch treated as if it were as fragile as a spider web.

When at last he did reach the floor, it took Kip a moment to realize that he could stand up and move in a normal way.

His breath came gusting out, and he told Farley, "I'm down. It's safe for you to get up and walk. You're only about three feet off the floor."

Farley got up and off the staircase as if he had been

scalded, and they both stood there shaking. But when the shock of their experience began to fade, Farley suddenly bolted for the door and ran outside. Kip chased after him, but tripped and sprawled. By the time he had picked himself up and gone outside, Farley was lowering himself into a crevice between the lighthouse and spit's end. Flying water almost obscured him.

Kip slowed down, half surprised and half amused. There were several such fissures. The lighthouse was supported not by one but by several massive slabs of granite; sea and weather had washed away the soil and enlarged the spaces between. But they did not go anywhere, and it was stupid of Farley to think he could hide there. Kip reached the boy just in time to grab him under the shoulders and pull him out. A wave broke and drenched them with spray.

Refusing to stand up, Farley groaned with disgust. "You practicing to be a cop or something? What's the big deal? Why don't you buzz off in your little boat?"

"Because there's something funny going on, and I want to know what it is! Now look, haven't you had enough?" Kip pointed at Farley's left eye, which was swollen almost shut. "You aren't going anywhere until you answer some questions, and I'll black your other eye if I have to!"

"You're scaring me to death." Farley managed a sarcastic smile. "You might be the one to get hurt."

Kip cocked his fist and brought his arm back. It was enough to make Farley flinch and change his mind. Bracing against another rush of storming spray, Kip crouched closer to the boy. Plainly cold, but probably stalling for time as well, Farley pulled a knitted navy-blue watch cap out of his pocket and pulled it over his head.

"All right, the sooner we get this over with the sooner we go home where it's warm and . . ." Kip stared at the watch cap, and to himself added, "Dark-haired!"

"What?" Farley looked up at him.

The clothes, too; out there in the light he suddenly realized that Farley was wearing pale blue denims, and the words exploded from him. "*You're* the lobster thief!"

Farley said nothing, but made a kind of "so what" gesture.

"Yeah, you're the one," Kip said, something else clicking into place. "And that hole, there . . . your boat is somewhere below, isn't it?"

"Took you long enough to find it out!" Farley almost laughed, and with obvious pride began to explain. "Just before you go around the point, there's a rock sticking up. And behind that rock, where it's hard to see, there's this place like a cave . . . wide at the bottom and real narrow at the top, where this crack comes in. It's big enough for a boat, even at high tide. Almost didn't make it today, though, because the water was too high . . . I had to lie down in the boat until it was all the way in, and then sit up and squeeze through the crack."

Picturing the point in his mind, Kip recalled the rock, and a suggestion of space, a shadow behind it. But he never had reason to wonder if something deeper than shadow was there. It was the same for the fissures around the base of the lighthouse. He remembered the first time he had ever walked out to the light and examined two or three of the holes. Having found them no more than shallow repositories for sand and sea-gull feathers, he had assumed they were all like that and of no interest. Apparently a city boy was more inclined to explore, having known little more than parks and sidewalks.

"What keeps the boat from floating out again?" he asked.

"It's tied to an old timber wedged in there," Farley told him. "Driftwood, I guess."

Kip nodded. "And so when you saw me coming, you'd run in there, crawl up through the hole and watch me from the lighthouse until I was gone. Right?"

"And boy, you looked dumb, always climbing across the rocks and looking for me out in the ocean!"

"It was pretty hard to figure," Kip admitted. "But what's it all about? Why steal lobsters? You didn't take enough to make selling worth while, and I don't think your family has trouble keeping food on the table."

Farley quit grinning, then. "I didn't steal them. Not really. I just took them out of the traps and let them go."

"You threw them back? Why?"

"To bug you, pal!" Farley spat sea water and bitterness. "Just to bug you and that old man! Remember how I wanted to try lobstering with you guys? But you couldn't see it. Just because I come from somewhere else . . . well, if I'm different, so are you!"

With that, Farley leaped to his feet and ran. Kip did not move to follow him until the other shouted over his shoulder. "I'm taking your boat . . . it's easier!"

Farley had enough of a head start that he might have made it to the boat. But either he had not seen Kip beaching it, or he had forgotten in the haste of flight that it was not in the usual place. He watched Kip more than where he was going, and then dropped to his knees to climb backward across the rocks toward water's edge—straight for the tidal pool and the whale.

Kip saw it happening, and for a long moment was frozen and unable to open his mouth; he did not want Farley to know. But if the boy fell in and frightened or angered the whale . . .

"Stop!" It burst from him, and he pointed. "Behind you, in the pool! Don't go that way!"

Farley hesitated, suspecting a trick.

"I mean it!" Kip yelled. "The boat isn't even there!"

His uncertainty growing, Farley stole a quick glance and saw that the boat was not there. And with that glance he also discovered how close he was to falling —looked down at the pool as he moved back from it, and saw in the rush of receding water that black and shiny back. Kip could not hide his dismay, and the other slowly began to smile.

"Now I get it . . ." he said. "Now I understand what's been going on! Those little games you've been playing out here . . . I've seen porpoises on TV. I know all about them!"

Kip shook his head. "That's not a porpoise. It's a killer whale, and . . ."

"I don't care if it's a polliwog! You've been trying to keep it quiet. Well, you know what's going to happen now? The whole stupid town is going to hear about it!"

"Listen, the whale's sick! Why cause it trouble just because you got a beef with me?"

"You're wasting breath, *pal!*"

And it was true. There was no arguing with him. Farley had the advantage, now. Smacking him in the nose or closing up the other eye would not have changed things in the slightest. Knowing all this, Farley quietly walked past him back toward the lighthouse to get his boat.

The best Kip could do was stand there helplessly, knowing that he and the whale no longer had the world to themselves . . .

CHAPTER 11

It did not seem reasonable to expect a crowd to gather on that kind of day. By then, the tide was falling, it was true; the swells had diminished somewhat, and the sea did not kick across the spit with its earlier ferocity. Anne was dying, and farther away. But those intervals of heavy rain had yet to cease, and the spit was still a bleak and bitter place. People came, though, wandering across dune and rock in twos and threes when the afternoon was still young. They gathered until there were perhaps twenty-five or thirty standing and gaping at the whale in its once secret refuge.

Earlier, Kip had returned to Potter's shack to dry his clothes and seek the old man's help and advice. But there was nothing to be done. There were no fences, signs, or laws to stop them. The old man did not even offer the encouragement of saying that, as Kip had wanted to believe, the weather might be on his side.

Potter's way of putting it was, "You can talk about giraffes and kangaroos, and the way a duck is put together, but men are still the strangest creatures on earth. You can't say that people will do this or won't do that. Human variety will make a liar out of you every time. That's the way it is, Kip. If that boy yells 'whale' in enough places, you're going to have people running out there even if it's raining green ink."

So he had gone back, and unreasonable or not, they came as the old man had said they would; came to gape and push until there were few places left on that narrow backbone of sand and rock where he could stand and still see the whale. They were rude in their curiosity, and so curious as to be unaware of their rudeness.

It was not bad, at first. Maybe it was because most of them were newcomers, the people who worked for the electronics plant. If they came from inland towns or where the sea was not an intimate part of their lives, Kip supposed it was adventure enough to stand where they were and look at the "monster" or at the "big fish," as some were calling it. Or maybe it was nothing more than surging water and the sharp confusion of glistening rocks that kept them from climbing down to the tidal pool. Whatever the reason, they held back and merely observed, and Kip began to believe that he had nothing worse to worry about than staying out there until rain or darkness sent them home again. For now, anyway. He was not thinking about tomorrow, the next day, or the day after that. This day, all by itself, had held quite enough.

But then a rock shot across short distance to thud against the whale's back. Kip did not move; it was too unexpected to be quickly believed, and neither did he understand the brittle laughter that rose here and there in the crowd.

Not having seen the one who threw it, he did nothing. And because it was such a pointless act, he ignored the sick feeling growing inside and dared hope that it would not happen again. But it was like watching a dark cloud, and feeling one drop of rain, and foolishly saying that no more would follow. A second stone flew, and then a third . . .

Kip broke loose from his disbelief and moved behind the crowd, watching until he saw someone bend down to pick up a rock. It was a boy his own age or a little younger. Angrily, he found a pebble just big enough to sting good and bounced it hard off the other's head. The boy shrieked, more startled than hurt, and turned to look at him with bewildered, tear-filled eyes. A woman next to him, apparently his mother, also turned around. Her eyes and mouth were wide with shock and sudden rage.

"Who are you throwing rocks at!" She shouted.

"Your son, I guess," Kip tried to keep his voice from shaking.

"Why!" The woman stepped closer, all bluster and red face. "What reason! Did my boy ever do anything to you?"

"No ma'am, he didn't. But that whale didn't do anything to him, either, and he threw rocks at it. Why?"

"That's different!" she sputtered. "And you know it! Roddy was just having a little fun!"

"Yeah?" Kip could not help himself. "What else does he do for fun? Squeeze canaries and crack turtles?"

He was surprised to hear people laugh at the remark, and the woman became almost apoplectic. She stood there gasping, shaking, and it took a great effort for her finally to point a finger at him.

"That's enough!" she said when she found her voice again. "I got a good mind to report you to the police!"

Kip was so furious that he shook his head and nearly laughed. "Lady, go right ahead! All I know is that your son was throwing rocks at a helpless animal. And if he does it again, I'll do it again, and it won't be a pebble next time!"

The woman came to the end of it, then. Not knowing what else to say or do, she grabbed at her son's hand and pulled him away from there. It was a preposterous sight—that dumpy spasm of a woman, all a-flap with galoshes and raincoat, jerking an oafish boy bigger than she was back toward the mainland.

Kip watched them go, glad, but with a certain feeling of added surprise. For all his life in Podquit, he had known people with faces that were not fashioned with beauty in mind—faces as knobby as summer squash, faces like broken granite, or as notched and sharp as an old axe. There was little prettiness in the burn of salt and wind, or in the weary, leathered hides of those who worked deep at the earth with plow and seed for a green-rising harvest. But he could not remember ever thinking of them, of any face, as being ugly. Not really. Not until now.

The crowd had diminished by two. But it was a small victory and short-lived. Before he could begin to breathe more slowly and end the shake of anger, there were four more—four young men throwing rocks and making a laughing game of it. Kip shouted and ran in front of them; tried to knock their arms down and make them stop. They were enough to push him aside quite easily. There was nothing he could do, and indeed, his efforts seemed to have made the game all the more amusing for them. And the whale could not move . . .

Helpless, Kip turned to the rest of the crowd and begged. "Somebody help me stop them! Please!" But they did not appear to see or hear him, and went on staring at that "big fish," the "monster." Somehow the four who had pushed him away without even being angry, and these others who were so deaf, were uglier than the two who had left—uglier, perhaps, because they would not respond or take him seriously one way or another. He nearly screamed in his frustration. "What's the matter with you people—don't you care? That poor whale is sick—and you act like it's a circus!"

"Peanuts, popcorn! Get your red-hots here!" A short, bullnecked man pushed his way to the front of the crowd. He climbed down on the rocks just in front of them and raised his hands. "Now in this ring . . ."

"Make them stop!" Kip yelled down at him.

"You're right. Okay, you guys, knock it off!" The man pointed a warning finger at the four who had been doing it, and Kip began to feel hope. But then the man's tones became mocking. "Really, fellows, you must stop dropping rocks on the poor fishy. Cease and desist whilst I render first aid."

With that, he went jumping down from rock to rock like some muscle-bound ape that had taken a couple of ballet lessons. Kip wished fervently that he would slip and go sprawling into the bay. It would have been some kind of compensation for that day.

As it was, that swaggering, posturing fool gained, the edge of the tidal pool. Unmindful of the water that rose and tugged at his ankles, he stared at the momentary rise of boiling foam and pretended to part it with his hands.

"Where are you, little fishy?" The crowd laughed, and when the interval of low water came and the whale could be seen again, he squatted down to take a closer look. "If you had a wrist, I'd take your pulse. But you don't have a wrist . . . or an arm . . . or a leg . . . run for your lives, it's the banana that stepped on Cleveland!"

His audience roared, and Kip found himself both disliking the man intensely and glad that he was there. That apish clown had no more concern for the whale than the rest of them, but at least, while he made comedy of the situation, no rocks were being thrown.

Perhaps the noise of the crowd had added to nervousness, and maybe it was nothing more than the pull of water that caused it, but the whale chose that moment to spout and to move a little with an easy slap of its flukes. To Kip it was a feeble effort. But to the man standing over the whale, it might as well have been the roar of a lion or a marauding elephant. He jumped back, nearly falling, and with terror in his face came scrabbling up to the top of the spit.

Before Kip could smile and think justice had been served, the man whipped out a pistol and fired four rapid shots at the whale.

For what seemed a terribly long time, Kip stood there gaping and unable to move. When he did move, he could not think—just saw the man standing there with the pistol still raised, and running, launched himself at him.

The impact struck the other down, but it was not enough to keep him down. He got up, and there was something in his face that had gone beyond anger. A fury, something wrong . . .

Kip saw it and came to his senses somewhat—enough to know that he was no match for this thick-necked man, and that he was about to be handed a brutal beating. But he was still too angry and sick over what had happened to think of backing off. The whale was dead, and he wanted to knock the man down just once more as part payment—just once more before the other had his way. Kip managed to step out of reach of the first swing, and to duck under the second. He stumbled on the rough ground, though, and saw his opponent closing in. But at that moment, another man came from somewhere and stepped between. In the confusion, Kip caught a glimpse of silver hair and realized it was Harper.

"That will do, Dorn," he said with a voice full of ice.

Dorn glowered at Kip with murderous eyes, but then turned and walked away.

The rain had begun again, and with the fight stopped, the crowd apparently decided the show was over; it began to break up and drift away as it had come. In a short while, Kip was left alone with his benefactor . . . this strange man who wore his raincoat like a cape and who, again, seemed both young and old.

Exhausted, Kip sat down on a slab of granite. "He would have killed me."

"He wanted to."

"Is Dorn crazy or something? And how come he stopped just because you told him to? He could've taken both of us on!"

"Dorn works in the stock room at the plant. He stopped because he's a very simple man with an almost childlike respect for authority. But crazy? No. He knows he's not smart, and it rankles—makes him insecure. He has to compensate for it, I suppose, by being loud and clowning around. That's what his little act down near the whale was all about. But the whale scared him, and you knocked him down in front of all those people . . ."

"But he killed the whale!"

"Oh, you were quite justified. You're not at all at fault, Kip. And listen here, your whale isn't dead."

"Dorn didn't miss . . ."

"No, but it was only a target pistol. Those bullets probably aren't much worse than bee stings to a whale with its thick hide and blubber. I'm sure that killing the animal was what Dorn had in mind, though, when he brought the pistol out here. Simple men are sometimes brutal . . ." Harper frowned in the direction of the whale and shook his head. "It would have been a blessing if he had succeeded."

"What?" Kip stood up and backed away.

"Kip, if you care about that whale, then you are going to have to face reality. The whale reacted very little to the two bullets that struck him. It's weak and probably dying—maybe in pain. You think about it, son. Those people and others will be back. More rocks will be thrown, and Dorn will probably sneak back here with his pistol. Your whale doesn't have a chance, and it won't know any peace for as long as it lasts. The stupidity of people, Kip—that's the worst kind of cruelty an animal can know."

"It isn't dying. I know it isn't," Kip told him. "I know because it's a young whale. It's going to be all right."

Harper pulled his collar up against the rain, and squatted down to look at the ground. "Perhaps it would have been all right if it had found a deserted beach somewhere away from people. Here, it doesn't stand a chance. It will die, and die very hard. Rather than have that happen, it would be best if I went and got my rifle. It's a heavy caliber and I could make a quick job of it."

Feeling the horror of it, Kip turned to meet Harper's eyes, but found only a weary kindness in them. There did not seem to be any arguing with the man. Maybe he was right—but Kip could not accept it or find an alternative, and so he lied.

"Then I'd rather be the one to do it."

Harper stood up. "I understand. But I'll be here in the morning. Saying good-by to a friend when that's the best thing for him—and especially being able to do what needs to be done here—well, it takes a special, grown-up kind of love, and I wonder if you could have found it yet."

CHAPTER 12

For a time, Kip remained with the whale and tried to find peace. They were gone now, all of them, and out of sight. How could it be understood? Even in the deep, abysmal gray of cloud and rain, and no matter the sound of a still-pounding sea, the spit was again as remembered. But the world was not. And why? What was it all about? The people who came there were human beings, and yet in some ways he could not recognize them . . .

Curiosity was something he could accept. It would have been much better if Farley Wilcox had not seen the whale, or at least had not involved it in his personal grievances. But, however annoying, it was still understandable for people to be curious; to come all that distance to stand and gape at a whale. Zoos never wanted for customers. And here, without bars to make it less novel, was an animal not often seen.

Kip huddled against the rain. It dripped from his face and might as well have been tears. *People*—and what kind, to throw rocks and shoot bullets? They came to the whale; not the whale to them, presenting some threat or danger. And perhaps worse, *people* standing there watching the rocks and the shooting as if such things were a normal part of a day. Yes, if merely a few were cruel, then what of the rest of them? That was the crux of it.

He shivered with cold and remembered the ugliness

he had seen. It seemed an obvious conclusion; there was no love in a flying rock or in minds that found no wrong in its being thrown. But where, he asked, would hatred come from? The whale was not a part of their lives. Books and pictures aside, it was an entirely new experience. They had no reason to think of it as they would a rattlesnake or a vicious dog.

Maybe it was just that they did not understand. Harper said Dorn was afraid of it, and maybe they all were afraid. Potter had said the whale belonged to another world; maybe that was why. And then, because it was no more than a "big fish," maybe they simply did not care. He did not know. But whatever the reason, the result was the same.

Kip wiped the rain from his eyes. It now seemed to him that growing up in Podquit and knowing its kind of people had been some sweet illusion. Apparently the world was not at all like that peaceful little bay, as he had believed, but more like the open sea—grand, no doubt, but given to treachery. And the world had come to Podquit.

He climbed down to where he could reach the whale, and in that interval when the water rushed away, touched his friend's back. The animal reacted, jumped in alarm or anger, recoiled from his touch as if his hand were a threat or could sting like remembered rocks.

"No!" Kip protested. "It's me . . ." But the water returned and he had to wait. When the dark back rose again through dropping water, he touched it again. "It's me." The whale still jumped, its tail thrashing, but Kip refused to take his hand away this time; kept it there even when the water came up to bury his arm and rush, slapping, against his face. And gradually the whale turned quiet.

But nearer to crying, Kip went back to where he had waited before, and wondered if the animal could ever really trust him again. Perhaps its quietness meant that it did, now; maybe it only needed a little time for that day to fade. And yet, where was there any time? *People* . . . people spoiled things.

Growing more dismal, he told himself that Harper might be right. Maybe killing the whale quickly would be a kindness. Both Harper and the old man had talked of its dying, while he had pushed the notion away to cling to the fact of its being young. But what did he know of whales, beyond the joy of this one? And no matter what was the truth of its sickness, this refuge had become a trap. As Harper said, people would be back and there would be more rocks and probably more bullets. Such things killed, sooner or later, and it was a hard way of dying.

Where the sickness was concerned, he could not make that kind of judgment, and he did not think anyone could or had the right. As for the rest . . . Kip still shrank away from it. It was a strange and convenient kind of logic—thinking it right for people to kill an animal to spare it from the cruelty of people. It made more sense, to him, for people to stop existing at the pointless expense of the life around them.

The only answer he could find to the dilemma was hardly an answer at all. The whale had to return to the sea, and since it seemed to lack the needed strength . . . well, it meant towing the animal, all three tons of it.

How did one even begin?

CHAPTER 13

Not much of the afternoon remained, but Kip hurried back to the old man's place. He was certain Potter could help. There was little that the ancient mariner, as he sometimes called himself, did not know. Fifty long sea-years were a great teacher.

But Potter would not even listen until Kip impatiently agreed to stand by the stove and drink tea while his clothes dried. Even then he listened as if he had heard the story before, and he made no comment on the idea of towing the whale out to sea.

"I don't suppose," Potter said, "you've thought of contacting the SPCA or talking to the Coast Guard."

"No," Kip admitted. "But I don't think there's enough time for that. Harper will be out there in the morning with his rifle. And there'll be a crowd again. Probably a bigger one if the weather is better. Besides, how do I know that the Coast Guard or the SPCA wouldn't take one look at the whale and decide the same thing that Harper did—that it ought to be put out of its misery."

"Well . . ." The old man noisily blew his nose. "Come to think of it . . ." He blew it again and blinked, watery-eyed. "The Coast Guard probably is on an alert basis until Anne is completely gone and the sea's calm again. You never know. Someone in trouble at sea . . . the possibility has to have priority over a whale. But don't you think you ought to give the SPCA credit for knowing a thing or two? And where time is concerned, how do you know they couldn't get here first thing in the morning?"

"Could you guarantee that they wouldn't decide to shoot the whale?" Kip almost shouted it. "Could you?"

"No, of course not! But if that's what they decided, then I'd be sure that it was probably the right thing to do."

"Yeah, well I wouldn't. I don't know what's the matter with the whale, and they wouldn't know either. And I don't think anybody has the right to decide whether something is to live or die unless they *do* know . . . even then, I'm not so sure, because how do you know an animal doesn't have a chance to get well again?" Kip turned and stared at the stove. "How do you know?"

It was a moment before Potter answered. "You're asking impossible questions. People can only try, and hope they are right. I don't know what else you can do."

Time was slipping away. Kip could feel it like a silent and rising wind in that room. He was afraid of it—of time, of that day and its people. The world was not as he remembered.

"We can take the whale back out to sea where it belongs," he said again.

Potter sighed wearily. "What am I going to do with you, boy? I told you how it was charted—that it couldn't last. But you grabbed and held on hard, and got yourself in pretty deep anyway. Lord, what an innocent you are! When are you going to learn that nothing is permanent? The world is like the tide. It isn't going to sit still just for you."

The old man went to the door and watched the sky and the rain, and said nothing for a while. Then, perhaps depressed by that dark and continuing downpour, he sat down again and frowned at Kip.

"You know," Potter went on, "it's a little like this town—expecting it always to stay the same."

"I don't see the connection," Kip muttered, wondering how long the old man was going to avoid the subject of towing the whale.

"I guess most folks saw it that way—cut off from everything by the sea and mountains. Some changes came, sure. Cars, electricity, a paper mill, and a shoe factory over in the valley, a few new buildings to replace the old. And motors instead of sails. Podquit changed just enough to survive . . ."

"It's getting late," Kip interrupted him.

"*But . . .*" Potter persisted, "it couldn't go on napping. The rest of the country . . . all this time we've been next door to a growing giant, and the day had to come when it'd need more elbow room. The electronics plant and its people—that's the first real footstep we've felt. And it's useless to quarrel with it."

Kip stormed away from the stove, losing what was left of patience. "All right! Okay! So what's that got to do with the whale?"

"Well, maybe it's a strange comparison to make. But the whale came and found a quiet place, and expected it to stay that way. And you thought it would, too, even though you were told. Being on the other side of the bay wasn't enough. It couldn't come that close to human society and not be touched, any more than Podquit could be near a growing country and not be drawn into it."

"Everything would have been all right if Farley hadn't seen it."

"*If!*" The word came exploding from the old man's lips. "And if it had come here and you were the only one to touch it, it would have died or gotten well and gone to sea and you never would have seen it again."

"You don't know that!" Kip refused to believe such a thing. "Besides, you forget Willy Tucker and that wild crow he found with the broken leg—fixed it up and made a pet out of the bird. Sure, it left, but it comes back every year, too!"

"Yes," Potter said gently, "I know. But the crow is part of the land and the forest—lives there on the mountain near Willy's place. The sea isn't like that, Kip. Leave the sight of land and you're not on this earth any more! You might as well be on the moon or halfway to Polaris, so don't talk about something here being the same! She's far, Kip, and there's a music out there that no one will ever understand. And the whale belongs to it."

"Well, how about those porpoises you see on television? They learn tricks. They're well-fed and happy . . ."

"That's right. They've adapted. And they are captives, every one."

Kip sat down, unable to believe or to go on arguing with the man. "I think what you're saying is that what's happened has happened, and I might as well sit back and do nothing . . ."

"You'd be wise to look at it that way." Potter stared at the floor. "But what I'm saying is that what you want to do you can't do by yourself, and I can't help you."

"Can't or won't?" Kip watched the door and felt sick.

"Both," Potter confessed. "I learned a lot of things in those years at sea. And when to come about and look for a quiet beach was one of them. When you've got too many years and miles under your keel, you begin to realize how mortal you are and that you have survived more out of luck than cleverness. Sailors and poker players, Kip—the luckier they get, the closer they are to running out of good cards to play. I'm sorry, but . . ."

"*You're* sorry! Boy, I must have been crazy to come here expecting to . . ." Angry and close to tears, Kip suddenly ran outside. He did not want any more of William Potter's fancy explanations. Time was running out, and the whale had to be returned to the sea. Somehow, quite obviously, he had to do it by himself . . .

CHAPTER 14

For a while, Kip did no more than wander aimlessly along the waterfront and search the confusion of his mind. He had not expected to find himself facing the task alone. And alone, how could he even begin? There were moments, indeed, when he looked toward the hill and thought of going home—of giving up and burying himself in his room with blankets and sleep. Potter had said that towing the whale to sea was something he could not do by himself. And regardless of how Kip felt about him now, he had to admit that the old man probably knew what he was talking about. But if Potter's words persisted and nagged, so did visions of what tomorrow would bring. They set him to wandering again, looking for the best way to begin. And there was no best way for him. Just one. He had to make do with what he had on hand, begin, and see if it worked.

Knowing that Potter would object and try to stop him, Kip sneaked back to the shed and very quietly started to gather the gear he thought he would need. The swells would still be slowly diminishing as the dying storm moved farther and farther away. But high tide was due at eight forty-five, and it was already after five. The water along the spit was rising; even now it was deep enough to cause difficulty. Thinking of that, and of the whale's tail, he had a vague, half-formed notion of how to deal with the problem. He took the line and marker buoy from one of the lobster pots, and added a boat hook. Then he filled the gas can, and because it would be getting dark soon, took the kerosene lamp down from its nail. These things he carried down to the beach where he had left Peabody's boat. That much done, he returned for the biggest and most important item of all—a hundred-foot coil of heavy manila.

The load was almost too much for the little boat, but it had to be carried only as far as the spit. Once the whale was in tow, the can of gas would be all he needed in the boat.

When he reached the spit, conditions were as Kip had expected. The swells were less, and the rising tide still low. He had to beach the boat as before, and carry the gear across wet, slippery rocks to where the whale waited. But it was only a matter of minutes before he was able to sit down by the animal and study a requirement that was both simple and difficult.

All he had to do was tie one end of the line around the animal's tail and the other to the boat. There was nothing complicated about that, but *doing* it would be something else.

Kip wanted to discover all the problems now, and not when he was in the water. He gave himself several minutes to consider everything, but still dreaded the decision to begin. How could he be sure? Time and light, however, were running short; it was very nearly dark enough, now, for him to need the lantern.

Without further delay, then, he found a ten- or fifteen-pound rock. Allowing maybe eight feet of rope, he tied the buoy to it and placed both at pool's edge, where they could be easily reached if needed. That done, he took one end of the towline and eased himself down into the water. Fighting that cold, heaving water probably was going to be the worst part of it, he knew. When it went foaming and boiling out between the rocks, for a few moments it would be about waist-deep. On the return cycle, he would have to tilt his head back to keep his nose out. And for almost all the time, the water would be pulling, pushing, threatening to knock him down and under. Fortunately, the way the whale's flukes were positioned, he would have a rock to brace himself against; it was not much, but it might spell the difference between staying put and having to get out.

Standing there spitting salt water, Kip knew his next move but was hesitant. The whale represented a certain danger to him. Everything had to be done with that fact kept in mind. The whale was his friend, but it was sick, and it was a wild creature that had not known the touch of a rope before. For all its intelligence, it probably would not understand. Whether it happened deliberately out of anger or with the defensive reflexes of fear hardly mattered. One slap of its flukes could kill him, and any sudden, violent change of position might find him between unyielding rock and three tons of moving whale. And so he talked when the water went down, and talked loud. After what had happened that afternoon, Kip wanted to be sure the whale knew who it was. Maybe the rope would be trusted, if it came with the voice of a friend.

"You aren't going to like this," he said, slowly moving his hand down the whale's back. "But you can't stay here." He went on talking, and gently touching the whale . . . gradually working toward the flukes. The floor of the pool, he found, was not flat. It sloped toward the bay, and also downward from its own edges. Every step toward the animal's tail took him into deeper water. Too deep, in fact, for him to pass the rope under even when the water was at its lowest.

Kip had suspected this might be the case, which was why he had brought the marker buoy and boat hook along. He had also thought, and confirmed it now, that when the water moved in and out with such force, the whale had to exert itself and swim a little to keep from being pushed around. It was not even swimming, but a slight rising and falling of the flukes.

He supposed he could get the rope under the tail when that exertion took place, if he went under himself. But not wanting in those circumstances to be blind even for a moment, Kip reached for the buoy and the attached rock. When the water went out, he pushed close to the whale and carefully decided where, on its opposite side, he wanted to drop the rock—not so far from the whale as to add to his difficulties, and not so close as to graze or hit the animal's tail—and let it fall.

It did what he wanted. The buoy rode the surface with its submerged line less than the length of the boat hook away. He did wish that he had tied it closer to the rock; it moved back and forth with the water, and traveled more than he liked. But feeling that the device would work, he decided to leave it alone.

Kip grabbed the boat hook and glanced skyward; darkness was falling. He had to work fast, and he had to be lucky. Pushing the hook at a downward angle into the water, he waited for that instant the water began to surge outward. When it came, he thrust the hook forward under the whale's flukes and searched for the buoy line. But before he could catch or even feel it, the whale settled again . . . and finding that strange, new object beneath it, suddenly raised its flukes and slapped down hard. Kip barely had time to push backward and out of the way. Scared, choking on the water he had swallowed, it took a little while to settle down and find the nerve to try again.

Quickly, he told himself. It had to be done more quickly . . . yes, he had to be sure that the hook was held at a right angle to the perpendicular, and when the moment came, make one fast sweep from right to left. Each attempt had to be limited to that, and no more.

Making ready with the hook, and watching for the right interval, Kip twice more probed for the buoy line. It was not until the fourth attempt that he finally sensed a resistance that was more than the tugging of water. Trying to be both careful and fast, he yanked hard and hoped it would find rock and rope on his side of the whale. Letting go with one hand, he cautiously reached for the hook—felt its metal, and then the twisted strands of manila.

Kip grinned, and wished he could go somewhere and sit down for a minute. But rest would have to wait until later, no matter what his nerves were doing.

The next step was to unfasten the rock and tie the buoy line to the heavy manila. This he did in a matter of seconds, and then climbed out to get on the other side of the pool. Stretching down, Kip grabbed the buoy, and when high water began to recede and make the whale work its tail, started pulling the line in. After two such intervals, the towline was under the whale and he had enough of its length to go around the animal and make a knot.

Bringing the rope back, slipping into the water and tying a bowline knot was easy enough. But he soon learned that he had best be out of the water when it came to drawing the loop tight. The whale reacted to it just as a wild horse would. Flukes sliced upward and raised mayhem, and it protested with its strange, ten-penny whistle of a voice.

Shaken badly, Kip retreated to the rocks and contented himself with tightening the loop a little at a time. He was cold, wet, and growing short of temper when he finally had it done.

The rest was simple by comparison, requiring only that he coil the other end of the line down on a rock at the edge of the spit, where it could be reached when he came back with the boat. There was a cleat on the stern for hoisting purposes or perhaps for pulling water-skiers, and it was just big enough to handle the towline.

Kip moved out from the spit slowly, until he felt all slack leave the line. Then he gradually opened the throttle. The boat danced, no more than a tethered toy. Not wanting it to happen that way so easily, he let the motor thrash for a minute more—as if dead weight could suddenly and inexplicably surrender.

But then he realized with bitterness how silly and unrealistic he had been. A little boat like this and three tons of whale, and what resistance that animal might be able to offer—it was preposterous! If he had stopped to think, instead of being so angry and impatient, he would have known the impossibility of it. Kip was too close to tears to laugh, but it was a laughable thing in a terrible kind of way. Yes, and being wrong here had spared him an even greater foolishness. He would have gone out to open sea in no better than a spoon . . .

Backing off on the line, Kip wondered what to do. He was not accomplishing a thing, but neither could he just go home and forget about it.

There was not another way of doing it. But he needed a much larger boat—something big enough not only to pull the whale but also overcome any attempts the animal might make to swim in the opposite direction. Even in its weakened condition, Kip suspected, the whale's strength was considerable. And the boat had to be big enough to be seaworthy.

He pulled alongside the bell buoy and fastened the towline to it for safekeeping until he could get back.

A boat, he thought, like the *Nereid* . . .

CHAPTER 15

Not wanting to attract attention to himself, Kip went the last two hundred yards to the dock with the motor barely turning over. By now the dock was most likely deserted, and so would be the waterfront street. Darkness was full, and rain fell again. But even so, a boat moving around would be an oddity and could not help arousing the curiosity of anyone who just happened to hear or see it.

He took the added precaution of tying Peabody's boat at the end of the dock, rather than taking it in to the beach, and from there walked no farther than a boat that was overturned and up on blocks for repairs. It was shelter and a place to hide away from the two lights that illuminated the dock. The lights had been put there years before for the tourist seasons, to discourage tampering with the boats. But now, because of all the new people in town, the lights burned every night of the year.

Kip shivered, dreading the hours ahead of him. He had not considered even for a moment asking Terrence Wilcox if he could borrow the *Nereid*. No matter how much the man seemed to like him, Wilcox certainly could not be expected to hand over the keys to a fifty-thousand-dollar cruiser, and it was just as unlikely that he would care to take the *Nereid* out himself at night in weather like this unless it was a dire emergency requiring the assistance of the Coast Guard Auxiliary.

It was possible, he supposed, that Wilcox would feel obligated to rectify a situation created by his son. But he would also be practical and insist on waiting until tomorrow. And by then the whale would probably be dead. No, he could not involve others without risk of losing all say in the matter. His anger and disillusionment aside, he could not seek the warmth of Potter's stove without endangering the plan. Neither could he go to his own home for dry clothes; his mother, even now, would be questioning his absence and perhaps trying to locate him by phone. That was the worst of it, her worrying, and not being able to tell her. She would never understand, and, frightened, would look for ways to stop him.

The best he could do was to wait with chattering teeth until it was safer to board the *Nereid*. Too, Kip wanted that ever-changing tide to be on the rise again when he went out to the spit.

Hours yet. And so much time had been lost already. Tomorrow was still tomorrow; night stood between, yes, and much had been accomplished, in that a towline was in place and ready to be used. But what if he could not get into the cruiser? What if he could not get its motors started? And what if the towline could not take the strain?

Kip huddled there, cold and miserable, and tried not to think of those things that could spell a whale's dying.

And they were like sea-angels, Potter had said.

He heard the clock strike nine in the village common. It was time to go; the tide was high. Studying for a moment the dock and waterfront, Kip went in a crouching run to the ladder and down to the *Nereid's* afterdeck. He was certain he had not been seen.

Thinking it might be useful in forcing an entry, he had brought a paint-scraping tool found while waiting under the boat. But since he perferred not to do any damage unless absolutely necessary, he checked around first and by chance found that one of the large ports forward on the starboard side had been left unlatched.

Crawling in and closing it behind him, Kip groped his way around the cruiser's bridge, searching for the flashlight that had to be kept there, somewhere, for emergencies. After several long minutes, he found it bracketed to the bulkhead only inches from where he had first come in.

Partly shielding it with one hand, he turned the light on and examined the controls. The wiring for the instruments and switches was completely enclosed by teakwood paneling, but a closer look revealed four screws where part of the paneling could be removed for access. He needed a screwdriver, then, and found one in a tool chest stored in a bulkhead compartment handily situated near the engine hatch.

It took only a short time to unfasten the panel and disconnect the ignition lock. When the ignition wires were twisted together, the instruments leaped into life, and another of his worries fell away. The fuel gauges indicated full tanks. Kip supposed it had been silly to wonder. Presumably any vessel that was part of the Coast Guard Auxiliary would always have a full load of fuel aboard. But he did not know Terrence Wilcox well enough to say that he was always prepared or that efficient.

Kip thought he heard something then and stopped, frightened, to listen. But the sound did not come again . . . if, in fact, there had been a sound at all. He knew that his nerves were all keyed up, and that his imagination would make the worst of nothing more than the creak of a mooring line. Dismissing it, he located the chokes for the engines, and the throttles. The latter had an interlocking device that permitted them to be operated as one or separately.

The moment had come, then; the time when he would have to risk being discovered. There was nothing discreet about the rumble of two powerful marine engines. But it could not be avoided, and setting the chokes, he thumbed the starter button. The engines turned, coughed and made him jump, but did not catch. Gas, he thought. The throttles had to be opened a little. Hesitant, reluctant to make yet another sound, Kip fumbled with the adjustment, and then, taking a breath, hit the starter again. The engines caught with a roar to crack the devil, and for a moment, frozen, he could only stand there and feel the *Nereid* tremble and strain against her lines. In slow motion, it seemed, he grabbed for the levers and backed them off until the engines subsided to an idle.

Kip leaned against a bulkhead, shaking and wondering if he had not aroused all of Podquit. But it was done, and waiting there in the dark would not change anything. Trying to hurry on unwilling legs, he left the cabin and went forward to cast off the bow line. Haste made him awkward, and the line was fat with rain, but he worked it off the cleat and made his way aft again to release the other one . . . and was startled to find William Potter there, leaning against the taffrail.

"I don't need your . . ." Kip began, and then stopped. It was obvious, in the old man's face and the way his fingers knotted around the railing, that he had not come to help. "How did you find out?" he asked, but did not care. "Leave me alone. I'm in a hurry."

Potter stared at him quietly and then folded his arms across his chest. "I've walked in the rain for hours, looking for you."

"Nobody asked you to."

"Your mother's worried. I told her you were angry at me and off sulking somewhere . . . that's how I had it figured, until I came home and the dock sounded like the starting line for a motorboat race. Kip . . . what do you think you're doing?"

"You know what I'm doing! I'm borrowing this boat, and I'm going to . . ."

"You're stealing it!" Potter cut him short. "And for what? Something you can't even do by yourself!"

"I can try!" Kip stepped toward the mooring line, but the old man came between. "Get out of the way! Don't make me fight you!"

"No, I'm not going to lift a hand."

"Then get off the boat and leave me alone!" Kip told him, so angry he was close to tears. "Go call the cops or something, but get off!"

Potter shook his head. "You'd be gone and across the bay before I could even get to a phone. All I can do is stand here and ask you to use your head—to listen to reason! Now suppose you kill those motors so we can talk this out."

Kip moved around him, toward the cleat, and reached for the line. "I'm going to the spit. You can do as you please."

"That's it?" The old man sighed.

"That's it," Kip told him.

"Very well." Potter pushed him toward the cabin and freed the line himself. Grabbing a boat hook, he held the *Nereid* away from the pilings. "Well? What're you waiting for? Get us out of here!"

Dumfounded, he hesitated, but then could only do as the man said.

The unaccustomed size of the cruiser was alarming, once given motion. But with a great deal of care, he nevertheless managed to turn the wheel and advance the throttles without ramming the dock or any of the boats that stood between them and open water.

Potter came in and joined him. "Relax," he grunted. "You might even try breathing."

Kip was too nervous not to smile, and decided he was more glad than angry. "She's so big."

"You'll get used to it. But if you're going to maneuver off that spit out there, best you start playing with the wheel now and find out how she answers."

Kip nodded and did some shallow turns on the way, but explained, "We don't have to go any closer than the buoy."

"That so? How are you going to move the whale? Whistle at him?"

"I've already got a towline on him, and the other end is tied to the buoy. Did it after talking to you. Peabody's boat wouldn't pull it," he said, and then asked, "How come you stayed aboard?"

Potter scowled at him. "It isn't as if I had a choice!"

"I gave you a chance to get off."

"Oh sure. And I would've been guilty of something worse than your stealing this boat! That would be fine, wouldn't it? A man with fifty years at sea standing by while some fool kid goes out and drowns himself!"

"I'm sorry. I didn't mean to drag you into it," Kip told him. "But I'm glad to have your help."

"Well," Potter said rather wistfully, "I suppose I've got a good card or two still up my sleeve somewhere."

"Are you really that superstitious?" Kip wanted to know. "All this talk about cards and luck . . ."

"No, not especially. But there is such a thing as luck, and I think a man's got only so much of it to his name. I should have been dead long ago—six torpedoings on the Murmansk run—and watching hull plates rupturing in a typhoon north of Guam. And when it comes to whales . . . it's something to have a harpooned 'blue' smash your boat to splinters and be sucked down five or six fathoms with no time to take a breath first. It was off the Norwegian coast, and I wasn't even twenty . . . all of that and a lot of other things. I'm an old man now, and I can't believe I've got much skin left on my teeth, that's all."

"Maybe," Kip said, "it isn't luck as much as it is knowing a lot and being a good sailor."

The old man smiled in the light of the instruments, but it was a tired smile caught in a face that seemed older tonight. "Sure, it helps to know, to be good at the things you do. But a man can be born to ships, he can take to them when he's still a weak and shaking thing barely out of his shell, and spend his life learning all there is to learn from keel to truck; he can sail the world around and become so much a part of winds and tides that he forgets how to walk on the land . . . and still he will never be an even match for that lady out there."

"Anne?"

"No, no . . . Anne is just a small part of it. The *sea*, boy. She's the biggest thing in the world. And when she begins to talk, then by God you'd better listen."

A few minutes more found them somewhere near the buoy. Kip could hear its eternal bell mourning away out there in the dark beyond the rain-streaked glass, but he could not see it.

"We're going to need light," Kip told him, cutting the engines to an idle. "There's a small searchlight on the top of this cabin."

"Good. The control handle must be on the overhead. But what about the switch?" Potter peered around in the dim glow.

"I don't know. If you can find the cabin lights . . ."

"No. We'd show up like a Viking funeral. Where's the flash . . . here, I found it," the old man said, but did not turn it on. "We'll use the searchlight just long enough to put us alongside the buoy. After that, the flashlight will have to do. I don't want some flap-eyed lubber seeing a light out here and reporting a vessel in distress to the Coast Guard!"

"Their base is miles from here," Kip pointed out. "We'd still have time."

"Yes, but they'd have Wilcox on the phone because of him being in the auxiliary."

"He can't do anything," the boy insisted.

"Nothing except gallop down to the dock and find his boat's been stolen! You'd make a lousy pirate, boy. You aren't thinking."

"It's just that I'd like to see what I'm doing. Coming up to the buoy with this monster scares me. And then we've got to stay by it long enough to get the towline aboard. That buoy might knock holes in us . . ."

"Well, listen to the bold mariner who was going to do it all by himself!" Potter turned the flashlight on, and pointed it at the overhead. "There it is. And the switch is on the handle. Fine."

Kip barely heard him. He was too startled by the way the old man looked in the reflected light of the flash. His face was flushed and worn and his eyes were bright with fever.

"You don't look so good."

"I don't look good even without a cold," Potter growled. "All right, now listen: We're maybe seventy-five or a hundred feet from the buoy. I want just enough turns on the engines to move us. When the buoy is about forty feet off our bow, I'll turn on the light. When that happens, you're going to bring her close and put the buoy at our stern. And hold us there. I'll be out there, ready. When I give you the word, you douse the light."

"But I don't know the exact direction from here. I've been guessing ever since we left the dock."

"You can hear the bell, so it wasn't a bad guess. There's not much direction to the sound in here, but if you'll stop drifting now and swing that compass rose back to reading somewhere between 95 and 100°, you'll be reasonably close to being right."

Kip did as he was told, but was not at all at ease with it. The sound of the bell grew louder and louder, until he was sure they were going to ram it in the dark. But when Potter finally turned the light on and swung its beam around, the red, swinging buoy was off the port bow and still a dim object in the rain.

"See it?" Potter got the windshield wipers going.

The boy nodded.

"Okay, then, move in. You might try cutting power when it's about twenty feet off the bow."

Kip worked against the swells, trying to hold a straight course. The best he could manage was an approximation, but apparently it was all right. Potter said nothing until it was time to cut power. Then the old man swung the beam around almost directly astern.

"I'm going out now. I want the buoy where the light is. When you see it, turn the light off."

"What if we go on by?"

"We shouldn't," the old man said. "But if we do, I still want that light out. I'll yell for reverse and work with the flash."

Potter took his station at the stern, and Kip listened as momentum died . . . listened to the loud bell and waited for that heavy, swinging mass to start slamming against the *Nereid*. But the sound moved from off the bow to amidship, and the buoy came into the light. He turned the light off, then, and quickly looked for the control that would give them power astern, and could not find it in the dim glow of the instruments. But the order for it did not come, and Kip watched the small beam of the flash dancing back there. Apparently, for all his time away from the sea and vessels bigger than a dory, Potter could still consider waves, current, and the displacement of a boat, and have some reasonable idea of how far momentum would carry.

The old man yelled then. "Towline secured! Hard to starboard now, and take up the slack easy!"

Kip spun the wheel and barely nudged the throttles. He could not tell if the *Nereid* was moving. But a minute later, Potter shouted again. "Rudder amidships!" And after that, "Fine. Now a little more power . . . a little more . . . more . . ."

After that, he could not hear Potter over the engines. But the feeling of motion had come almost suddenly, and a quick wave of the flashlight warned Kip from adding more power. The old man came back into the cabin, drenched and still breathing hard. The grimness in his face was deeper. Seeing this, and feeling nothing in *Nereid* to suggest that it was pulling three tons, Kip was certain the line had snapped. Indeed, Potter wearily reached for the throttles and eased off on the power a little.

"What happened?" Kip asked. "Did the line . . ."

His friend gestured for silence, seeming to count in his mind, but then saw the chronometer and stared at it. "All right, bring her back to about one-two-five degrees. That should take us safely past the light. And I'd hold it at seven knots or so."

Kip swallowed hard. "You mean we've done it?"

The answer came soon, but not from Potter. *Nereid* began to plunge and rise in the long, rolling swells of the open sea. It was nearly ten o'clock.

Maybe the old man had said nothing, Kip thought, because he was thinking about a deck of cards . . .

CHAPTER 16

Behind the line of dunes and granite forming the bay, and in the dark, the world had seemed far enough away; people, warmth of lights, solid earth. But here there was nothing, nothing until England, as Potter had once said. They saw only the green glow of instruments and the black squares of glass in which their own faces were reflected. The sea, though, could be felt, and its immense, empty distances sensed. It did not make a difference, knowing that Nancy's Light was only a few minutes astern.

"Let me take the wheel now," the old man said.

What they had been doing seemed to have taken so much out of Potter that Kip could not ignore it. "Why don't you go down into the forward compartment and stretch out on one of the bunks for a while? This thing sleeps five or six people, you know."

"I want to stay up here where I can keep an eye out."

"What's there to see? It's dark. Nothing but water. We won't be in any shipping lanes, will we? You're sick, and I can handle it all right."

"A bad cold isn't going to sink me," Potter told him. "Now scoot off that dentist's chair and go check the towline. I've got a switch to find. We ought to be showing running lights."

There was no arguing with him. Kip got down and

stood aside with misgivings. That high, one-legged chair was bolted solidly to the deck and had arm rests, but for all that, the old man still was less than steady.

Kip took the flashlight and went outside, moving cautiously across the rolling deck. He crouched at the stern, and bracing himself against the taffrail, pulled on the line. Not able to move it, he knew the whale was still in tow. Both the knot and the cleat to which the line was made fast were in good order. Kip pointed the light astern and looked back along their wake, but could find neither the whale nor the added turbulence that would mark its position. The light was not strong enough.

Working his way back to the cabin, he saw the running lights come on. They burned on the uppermost part of the *Nereid's* bridge, port red and starboard green. Above, on her antenna mast, another small light was like a near and wild star, a bright pendulum sweeping across blackness with the cruiser's rolling.

"The lights working?" Potter asked when he came in.

"Yes. And the line looks all right. But what about the whale . . . does it hurt him to be towed backward like this?"

"Don't see why it should. As long as he can get air when he needs to, that's all that's required." The old man coughed deep and hard, and then fought for breath.

Kip waited a moment and said, "That's what I mean. Can he come up, going backward? Do you suppose he's strong enough?"

"Towing keeps him close to the surface; I imagine his blowhole is out of the water most of the time. But even so, he's strong enough. Didn't you feel it? After we took the slack out of the line and began to pull . . . how nothing seemed to happen, and then the boat moving suddenly? The whale was pulling against us at first, and then gave up."

"I didn't know that's what it was."

The old man swung off to the northeast, and silence fell for a little while. The rumble of the engines and the constant pitch and roll of the cruiser riding across the swells was nearly hypnotic. Too, they were both tired. Kip sat down with his back against the bulkhead.

It was an odd thing to feel; to look around, to listen, to think about having the *Nereid* underway. The crime of taking it was, to him, still overshadowed by necessity. But even so, the *Nereid*—fifty thousand dollars' worth of plush cruiser. Kip remembered the time, not long after they'd met, when Farley took him aboard to show him around. Accustomed, like Potter, to rugged and practical boats designed for work, he had been astonished by the opulence of what he saw. More than the Wilcox home, the cruiser emphasized the difference between their two worlds. For him it was not a matter of concern, but Farley had become almost apologetic by the time the guided tour was finished. And why apologize for the good life?

"You know," Kip said, "I still don't understand why Farley did it—messing around with our lobsters and telling everyone about the whale. Why did he feel like he had to get back at me?"

"Because you wouldn't give him a job with us."

"Yeah . . . but I explained that there wasn't enough money for three people. And he didn't need money. Did you know his weekly allowance is more than what I make working?"

"It figures," Potter said. "Didn't it ever occur to you that his always having a fat cargo might be the answer to your question?"

"How do you mean?"

"I mean making money wasn't really what he had in mind."

Kip was puzzled. "What else could it be?"

"Well . . . let a kid take root . . . where was it, New Jersey? A place that's roaring all the time—big industry, lots of people, lots of things to do. Let a kid grow and be shaped by it . . . and then pull him out and drop his anchor in Podquit. What do you suppose it's like?"

"Pretty strange, I guess."

"Strange is the word, boy. It's like being moved to a foreign country. Even the people are different. We all use the same words, but it isn't the same language. And when did we ever make these people feel welcome? When they first came, we acted like they were under a yellow flag—like it was a cholera ship come into the bay. We tolerate them now, and that's all. And because the difference between us is mutual, it will be a long time before it all blends together—before we get to be a little like them and they get to be a little bit like us. Do you see what I'm getting at?"

"No . . ."

"What I'm saying, boy, is that Farley wanted to fit in somewhere. He wanted to belong and be a part of this new place. The money didn't matter."

Remembering something, Kip turned silent. The visit to Farley's home—he had gone there late in the morning to meet the boy's parents and have lunch with them. Farley, as usual, had not had much to say, and his mother had spent most of the time sailing back and forth between dining room and kitchen because, as she had said, they had not yet found a maid. It was not something he had paid much attention to at the time, but Kip recalled that there had seemed to be a kind of perpetual impatience between the boy and his parents—something that fell just short of brusqueness. And on top of all this, Terrence Wilcox had asked question after question about lobstering; the man had been frank in his admiration, and had treated him more and more like an old friend.

"Saving for college, huh? Good! I like to see a boy set a goal for himself and work hard for it. Hard work and a solid education—it builds a boy's backbone."

It had been a little embarrassing, but Farley had seemed pleased by their reaction to his guest, and so the visit had gone well enough. But then Mr. Wilcox had announced that it was after one and he had to return to the plant. Farley's mother was going somewhere to play bridge.

Kip remembered standing up and saying, "I've got to go, too."

"You're not staying?" Farley's jaw had dropped.

"The dory's motor quit on us yesterday, and we're getting it back this afternoon. Potter and I have to go out and tend to the bed."

"But I thought . . ." Farley had begun and then stopped, obviously disappointed.

"Now, listen here." Terrence had paused long enough to put on his jacket. "Kip had lunch and visited with us, and now he has to go back to work. And it's no reason for you to start fussing!"

"Yes, dear," his mother had said, "why don't you go see a movie? It would be a nice walk, and . . ."

"Alone?" Farley had complained. "No, thanks."

"I imagine there will be other youngsters at the theater." She had smiled. "Some you met in school probably."

"I don't know any of them."

"And you won't get to know them sitting here," his father had said, and left.

Farley had shrugged. "Well, I've got an airplane model to finish." And with that he had turned and gone to his room.

The *Nereid*'s instrument panel came back into focus, and Kip got up to look at the compass for a moment. Still northeast. . . . He had not understood what that visit had revealed, or really thought about it much until now. But what Potter said seemed to fit.

"You're probably right," Kip told him. "Farley wanting to belong, I mean. But if the money didn't matter, why did he act as though it did?"

Potter squinted at the chronometer above the windshield. "I'm not sure—except that if he wasn't paid, he wouldn't be like anyone else. He wouldn't really be a part of it that way. On the other hand, if he asked and you let him work for nothing—well, wouldn't he still feel different, like he was nothing more than a guest all the time?"

Kip began to see some logic in it. "I guess *I* should've asked him if he minded working for nothing. Does that add up? I mean, not feeling like a guest that way?"

The old man nodded. "That might have been the thing to do. It would have given him a choice, anyway. But tell me: can you imagine yourself asking someone to work for nothing?"

Kip thought about it for a minute. "No, I guess not. It would bother me."

"You see? Good old New England propriety. So busy being right and proper, you don't see the real need."

There was nothing Kip could say to that; he supposed it was true. Getting up, he went outside again to check on the towline.

In the thin beam of light, he was surprised to see the line pointing not astern but off to the port side. Following outward with the flash, he caught the barest glimpse of a fin slicing through the water. The whale was swimming, moving along with the *Nereid* under its own power. Hurrying inside, he told Potter about it.

"Sounds like he got tired of riding backwards. And maybe his bellyache, or whatever it is, is getting better." The old man smiled. "I just hope he doesn't come too close and foul the screws with the towline."

"Isn't it about time to turn him loose and go back?"

Potter looked at the chronometer again. "We've been underway for half an hour . . . no, forty minutes . . . and making seven knots. That puts us about five miles from the light. I don't know how long your friend can keep it up before he weakens again, but he's swimming pretty good. I think we ought to keep going for a couple hours more. That would give us twenty miles and less chance of finding a whale in the bay by morning."

"I hadn't thought about that," Kip said. They were farther out even now than he would have gone by himself.

"I didn't think you had." The old man could not help the sarcasm. "And I don't suppose you thought about how to turn the whale loose, either."

"No," Kip admitted.

"And you were going to come out here all by your-self!" Potter would not let it alone. "Kids are crazy; that's all there is to it!"

"I would've cut the line, I guess," Kip said.

"Well, if he won't hold still long enough for us to get the boat hook under that loop, we may have to do just that. But I don't like it that way. There's no telling how long the whale would have to go with a fathom or two of line dragging behind. It'd loosen or rot away eventually . . . but maybe he will be tired enough not to give us a struggle."

Potter was silent for a moment, and Kip stared at the chronometer, watching the second hand's slow sweep around the dial.

"You *did* make a loop that could slip, didn't you?" Potter asked.

"Well, sure," Kip said rather testily. "I'm not *that* crazy."

Potter had stopped talking after a while, stopped listening, ceased even to acknowledge with a nod anything that was asked or said. The old man simply went elsewhere in his mind . . . perhaps to sit very much alone with this sea that was his love and his fear. Gradually, there *was* more of a sea, and more wind in the rain that hammered against glass. It had been expected, though. They were, after all, drawing closer to a dying storm. And so maybe silence had come of fatigue and not feeling well. Kip did not know; Potter's face was a mask haunted by both fever and preoccupation.

But there was a surrendering, a certain weariness in the sudden way Potter reached for the throttles, now, and reduced power until the *Nereid* held position and no more.

Kip glanced at the chronometer questioningly; they were nearly twenty minutes short of the intended two hours' travel. "I can take it the rest of the way," he said, "if you want to lie down."

"No, this is good enough. Go out and see where the whale is."

Sea and weather seemed even worse when he went out with the flashlight. But there, of course, he could feel the wind. And without headway, the *Nereid* was more abrupt in its motions. Pointing the light around, he saw the whale on the surface, about sixty feet away and almost directly astern. It was harder to see the animal this time, even that close, and he realized that the wind was strong enough now to make spindrift. The swells were no longer glassy.

Kip went back to the cabin door to tell Potter the whale's position; he almost had to yell.

"All right," Potter said. "Sounds good. I'm going to put this thing in reverse, and as we back in you've got to pull the line aboard. You're going to have to signal me with the flashlight to keep me on course—blink it to make me stop."

"Where do you want the whale?"

"Right where we put the buoy when we took the line aboard."

Kip nodded. "Don't you want the searchlight on?"

"When we've got the whale alongside. Until then I'll be too busy with the wheel and watching you to stand up and keep aiming that thing."

Kip returned to his place at the taffrail. The *Nereid*

slowly began to move backward. Giving signals with
the light until Potter was aimed right, Kip began pulling
in the heavy, water-soaked line. It was hard work and
it had to be done fast; he could not fall behind for long
without danger of the heavy manila drifting into the
propeller blades. He paused now and then, but only for
long enough to signal Potter back on course. When the
whale was just astern on the port side, he blinked the
light. The old man brought the cruiser to a stop and
gave it forward power again to hold the position.'

By pulling on the line, Kip managed to keep the whale
and cruiser from drifting apart. But it was not going to
be easy, with that pitch and roll, to catch the loop with
the boat hook.

The searchlight came on and swung around to center
on the whale. Potter joined him with the hook and
nodded as Kip continued to pull on the line. "Keep him
right there, and as soon as I grab hold with the hook,
give me slack."

The old man put one leg through the railing to brace
himself and aimed the hook, trying to match his thrusts
with the *Nereid*'s heaving. Effort after effort failed, and
Potter's strength was going fast.

"The sea's getting worse," Kip yelled.

"Yes!"

"Want me to try?"

"I'm all right!" the old man yelled back and stub-
bornly went on with it, reaching farther and farther with
the hook until Kip was certain he would fall overboard.

The rain came harder, and with a sudden and violent
gusting of wind, blew sideways as if up and down had
ceased to exist. Kip watched it, startled, and somewhere

something snapped and sang for an instant. He turned to search it out, but then Potter yelled.

"Slack, Kip! Give me slack!"

The boy quickly fed the line over the side, and Potter straightened up with a hard jerk.

"The whale's free. Bring in that line . . . no, throw it overboard! There isn't time to secure it!"

Kip did as he was told and hurried after Potter to regain the shelter of the cabin. There, Potter threw the boat hook down as if he had not realized he still carried it, and grabbed the wheel. Advancing the throttle and bringing the *Nereid* about, he shook his head and glared at the blackness beyond the glass.

"I hope we still have time, boy! I hope we have time . . ."

"What's happened?" Kip felt the cruiser slamming through the water. "Why are we going so fast?"

"That's *Anne* out there!"

CHAPTER 17

Anne . . . only hours ago, back across that long day, Kip had thought of her as being something distant and retreating—a far anger that caused nothing more than rain and higher than usual tides. Even when she was still coming and had yet to pass them by, he had seen her as part of an indefinite future and another day. But now the name crashed across the mind and numbed it.

Kip was bewildered. "I thought she was dying!"

"Well, she's changed her mind again, and she's headed for the coast! Here, take the wheel." The old man slid off the seat and went to the radio transceiver, which was built into the cabin's starboard bulkhead. Turning the light on, he squinted at its knobs and dials and quickly threw a switch. When the radio warmed up, he boosted the volume and moved the needle across the various frequencies; the speaker hissed with static and that was all. Making sure it was set for receiving and not transmitting, Potter tried again, but had the same result.

"Seems dead . . . maybe the antenna is down. Something's wrong . . ." The old man pounded it with his hand.

Kip suddenly remembered. "That's what it was!"

"What?"

"When we were turning the whale loose and those first

hard gusts hit us . . . I heard something snap and sing. But you yelled for slack then and I forgot about it."

"That's it for the radio, then." Potter turned it off. "We can't send or receive."

"Can't it be fixed?"

"I don't know, but I'm not going to risk one of us being washed overboard just on the chance that the other *might* be able to yell mayday. We're on our own, and I'm afraid it will have to stay that way. But at least I can get an idea where the storm center is."

The old man went outside, just beyond the door, and Kip watched him turning this way and that, apparently determining the direction of the wind. A moment later he raised his arm, sighted along it as if aiming a pistol, and then came in to consult the compass.

"Northern hemisphere . . ." Potter seemed to be remembering something out of a book, "with wind directly on the face . . . puts storm center about ten degrees to my right. Allowing for where we've gone, and where she was last we heard . . . well, we're somewhere on her northwestern edge. And we know about how big she is, so her center is thirty or thirty-five miles . . . almost off our port beam. I don't know her exact line of travel yet, but it doesn't make much difference to us. In this gold-plated bathtub, we're in for a bad fight. Wind must be hitting fifty or so in the gusts even now, and the closer she gets . . . it'd be near a hundred close to her eye, maybe more."

Kip looked back at the ports at the rear of the cabin, as if Anne could be seen in that blackness. "Maybe we can outrun her."

The old man shook his head. "If she's like she was

before, her forward speed is fifteen or twenty miles an hour."

"But the *Nereid* will go much faster than that!" Kip protested. "Thirty knots, I think!"

"Sure . . . in calm water. A couple of minutes ago, you wanted to know why we were going so fast. Take a look at the gauge, there. Eight or nine . . . not much more than what we were doing with the whale under tow. And that's about the best we can do without pounding to pieces. The sea's changed that much, boy! Anne's gaining on us all the time. We can hope to make the bay before she gets strong enough to do us in. And that's all we can do! Hope."

"I still think we could go faster," Kip told him. "This isn't a little runabout, you know!"

Somehow Potter nearly managed to laugh. "Yeah, big and mostly glitter. A fair-weather boat, Kip. Meant for parties alongside the dock and fishing on Sunday, not for something like this . . . which is why . . ."

"Why what?" Kip asked, and then turned to see the old man swaying on the seat, his eyes closed. "Hey . . ."

"It's all right. Just a little dizzy . . . you don't suppose an old salt like me is going to get seasick, do you?" He straightened up and shook his head like someone trying to stay awake. "I was saying . . . which is why I'm not coming about to take the sea under our bow. The *Nereid* would ride better if we did. But I don't want to do that unless we have to, because we'd be committed to the storm for certain then. No, we'll run with the sea for as long as we can get away with it. It's a gamble . . . maybe it will give us time, and maybe Anne will turn. Then again, maybe it's for nothing. Who knows? But it's a better gamble than trying to play a hurricane's game with this toy."

"Like playing poker," Kip said. "You're waiting for a better card."

Potter nodded, something terrible in his face.

It was not a time for talking. What had been said, had had to be said, and they fell silent after that. It was a time for holding on and fighting the wheel, and though they were still too far away, watching for the lights of Podquit. The dock lights were always on, of course, but very probably the town would be brighter than usual. Neither Kip nor the old man had been around a radio to catch the first reports of Anne's coming to life again, but the villagers would have heard and started preparing for it. The whole town would be up and keeping vigil.

They were too far away, but they watched, hoping, just the same. To see the lights, to see just one burning through all that driving rain and spray would mean that they were close enough to make it home. And all the while, Anne gained on them.

The changes were not swift; there was only a slight difference between bad enough and worse. From the moment they freed the whale and turned to run, the *Nereid* had at intervals been taking sea across her stern. Now it happened a little more often and with a little more severity. It was this, if it became bad enough, that would force them to come about and give up the race for home. And so they listened for its happening, and gauged how it felt, and went on with that mad, roller-coaster ride.

The whale . . . there had been no time to think about it, to wonder. It would have gone deep, yes. Far below this raging. But what about its illness, and the threat of enemies? He had not even had time to feel sadness or to be glad at having delivered the animal from the cruelties of people. It was hard to remember other moments, to get away from the one at hand. Anne overwhelmed everything with her screaming . . .

It sounded like a million people dying—winds full of voices. Maybe, Kip thought, this was what Nancy Makem heard the night she died—this sound of agony . . .

The cabin door burst open, then, and the sea came rushing in. Potter yelled something and turned on the cabin lights. But Kip could only stare. The deck was under a foot of water. Some had filled the hatchway leading down to the forward compartment; fortunately, that door was closed. The rest of it, though, surged wildly from side to side, and when the bow rose again, raced for the door, but forced it shut before much could escape.

Potter yelled at him again. "Get that door open so it'll run out! And then brace it shut with something! Try the boat hook!"

Kip struggled across the crazy pitching of the deck with water tearing at his legs and finally managed to reach the door. He got it open just in time to catch the bow coming up again and held on for dear life while the water fought past him and through that narrow opening. The next fall of the bow found most of it gone. Kip slammed the door, jammed the point of the boat hook deep into the wood near the latch and wedged the other end hard against one of the cabin's built-in seats. The inch or so remaining flowed into the hatchway, through which some water had already seeped into the forward compartment; there was not enough to cause them trouble down there.

"It's all right, now," he told Potter. But just as he said it, the engines died.

There was no question as to what had happened. The water had been trapped in the cabin long enough to leak into the engine space. The hatch giving access to the motors was just inside the door, and being in an enclosed area and not on the weather deck, was anything but watertight.

"Get a rag!" Potter shouted. "Get those plugs and wires dry fast or we're dead!"

There was no time to look for rags. Kip ripped a curtain from one of the ports and jerked the hatch open, shouting, "The flashlight! And below you . . . pull the wires apart!"

Potter turned and threw the flashlight, and the boy sprawled on the deck and started wiping the water off the ignition system as fast as he could. The result of losing power was immediate and chaotic. The old man did as much as could be done with the wheel, but it was far from enough. Staggering under the explosive force of sea and wind, the *Nereid* was almost completely out of control. At any moment it could be caught beam to an oncoming sea and capsized, or take too much under the stern and go too deep at the bow to recover.

"Blast you, boy! Hurry!"

Kip did not even try to reply. There were sixteen plugs and a wire for each that had to be dried while he fought the insane motions of the cruiser. More than once the motion caused him to pull a wire loose, and time was lost connecting it again.

The cruiser took on a crazy tilt, listing deeply to star-board. It tore Kip loose and he rolled hard against the bulkhead, yelling out with surprise. For an age, the *Nereid* held there unable to answer to the weight of its keel. Potter was knotted over the wheel, frozen to it with all his strength.

"Can't wait . . ." the old man gasped, and Kip crawled forward and lunged the last few feet to grasp and con-nect the wires again. Potter thumbed the button and the starters began to grind. The engines turned, coughed . . . and miraculously caught hold. It was a ragged chorus, at first. Not all the cylinders were firing. But it was power, and the sound was beautiful. The cruiser began to respond, and Potter fought it out of the list and around to run with the storm again. After a few moments, each of the motors was firing on all eight again.

"Lord Almighty," Potter said.

Kip closed the engine hatch and sat down, slumped against the bulkhead. "We'll make it yet."

The old man smiled weakly. "I don't know, Kip. I don't know . . ."

In spite of Potter's doubt, they went on and seemed to hold their own. The hurricane did not appear to be getting any worse. Perhaps Anne was turning once more, or maybe she did not have the forward speed they had anticipated. Or again, maybe changes for the worse were too easily disguised by conditions that were already des-perate. It was a little like freezing to death at forty below zero; minus forty was quite enough, and having it drop gradually to fifty was not going to be terribly obvious.

No, everything seemed to have stabilized. The motors

ran, and the cabin door held against those occasional seas that came breaking over the stern. And minute after minute went by until violence and danger reached a state of being both frightening and monotonous. But still there was not a single spark of light to be seen ahead.

"Shouldn't we be seeing Podquit by now?" Kip had stared until his eyes watered.

"I think so . . . enough time has passed. But . . ."

"But what?"

"Well, I can't be sure. Our indicated speed can't be depended on because we're getting pushed around too much. I don't know that we're still on course . . . I've allowed for drift, but it's a poor guess at best. I don't know . . . maybe it's just the rain, and we'll see lights in another minute or two. And maybe it's worse than that. Maybe . . . Kip, turn the searchlight on and aim it straight ahead."

Kip did as he was told, but asked, "Why? What good is it?"

"I just thought of something . . . suppose the wind has knocked Podquit's power lines down? We could be off the entrance to the bay and not see a thing. And if we've missed, there's still a coast there somewhere and an awful lot of rocks . . ."

The thought would have been chilling enough even on a calm night. But to approach an unseen and rugged coast line when the sea ran wild . . . Kip anxiously stared down that short, rain-killed beam and watched for the glistening of dark, beleaguered rock. But he could barely see beyond the windshield.

"I don't know . . . maybe I ought to be up on top

with the light where I can see farther," he said, although the thought of trying to hang on up there was alarming. "This way we wouldn't be able to turn in time, would we?"

There was no answer from the old man. Kip repeated his question and then turned to find him slowly slumping over the wheel. Crying out, Kip grabbed at Potter and kept him from falling—eased him off the seat and down to the deck. It was the best he could do. There was not a prayer, in that careening boat, of getting him below into the forward compartment. And the wheel could not be left even for that long, anyway.

Kip seized the wheel and fought the *Nereid* back on course. "What's the matter?" he yelled at the old man. "Are you all right? What happened?"

Potter did not move. His eyes flickered open for a moment, and his voice was almost lost in the storm. "You've got to do it now . . . keep a sharp lookout . . ." The words were a struggle. "If it gets worse, you've got to come about . . . remember . . . come about . . ."

The old man's eyes closed again. And Kip did not know whether he was still alive.

CHAPTER 18

Words echoed. *You've got to do it now* . . . yes, it was all up to him, and never before in his life had Kip felt so alone or so inadequate.

He kept glancing down at Potter's prostrate form, wishing that he would move . . . that his eyes would open again . . . that he would, in another minute or so, sit up and say that a little rest was all he had needed . . . that, if nothing else, he would show some small sign of being alive. But such signs were lost, if they existed at all, in the violent motions of the cruiser.

You've got to do it now . . . how? The old man had kept the cruiser's stern to the oncoming sea. Kip knew this, but could not see the direction of the waves; the searchlight's narrow beam, for the short distance it reached, revealed only confusion. What he needed to learn had to be felt, and he had never piloted a boat in a storm. Obviously, if the stern came out of line, unchecked, the *Nereid* would very quickly take the sea more and more on its beam and be in danger of capsizing. But how in all that insanity could he even feel it begin? The compass was of no use in this respect; its rose was never still. It was hard enough, in that constant spinning off to port and starboard, to find the compromise that represented the course home . . . if that course was still good.

How? Potter had had fifty years in which to learn. And if it had to be done, where would he find the courage to turn away from the dreamed-of harbor, its lights and solid shore, and point straight out to sea again?

Kip would have wept with his questions and fears, if there had been time.

But Potter did not move—looked dead—and there was no time for anything except fighting that wheel with tentative hands, and following the flights of the compass, and watching a drowning world through swimming glass and sideways rain for the rocks and coast that might be left. And the wind seemed stronger . . .

Kip didn't find the coast or see any hint of lights out there. Perhaps Potter had guessed the truth when he'd said that Podquit's power lines might be down. But too much time had passed, and while it was not noticed at first, it became increasingly difficult to stay on course. Ultimately, as near as he could figure it, he was being driven on a heading of roughly 225°. It did not take much of a navigator to know what this meant. The *Nereid* was probably south of Podquit Bay, and definitely running parallel to the coast. Glancing desperately at Potter, he wished the old man could somehow tell him what to do . . . what to expect.

Kip searched his mind, trying to remember anything Potter might have said about the hurricane. And the best he could manage came not from Potter but from a vague kind of common sense. Anne spun around her center, and so the *Nereid*'s heading would continue to change—become more and more southward until it found him pointed away from the land. But at the same time, Anne was also moving forward toward the coast . . . and he did recall then that Potter had mentioned drift, meaning that the *Nereid* was to some degree being carried landward. But how fast? Not as fast as the storm; every minute meant the cruiser was deeper within the hurricane and closer to its center . . . and closer, its turning would be more rapid and its winds more violent . . . yes, he thought he remembered that much. But what good was it to know? And what good was it to go on running before the sea with home already lost and behind them?

Kip carefully began to turn the wheel to bring *Nereid* about. It would not bring them back up the coast to the bay; hope for that was gone. But control would be easier. Indeed, *Nereid* had barely begun to answer the helm when he discovered that it was probably time to make that maneuver anyway. Wind and sea had been growing worse, but more than he had realized. *Nereid* plunged downward into the trough, and, beam to the oncoming crest, listed sharply to port. Kip eased off on the wheel, but she refused to answer and the list sharpened . . . he saw water slide along deck's edge until the bottom of the railing was awash. A degree or two more and *Nereid* would capsize. Terrified, he punched the throttles open, and with more power, the cruiser at last began to recover. Kip fought her around, eased the throttle, and slumped over the wheel to find his heart again.

It was less of a fight, then; control came easier, for a while at least. But he was tired, and at the end of another hour was coming close to the end of his strength.

It was shortly after that, that he first noticed that the

cruiser was beginning to feel strangely heavy and as if
it were shuddering more when it rose out of the troughs.
For a while, he blamed his own fatigue; to arms about to
fall off, anything would have felt heavy. But he could
not dismiss the fact that he felt it through more than the
wheel.

A small and growing chill sitting at the back of his
mind, Kip finally dared consider tying off the wheel for
a moment; there was a fancy, bright-colored loop of
nylon attached to the instrument panel for that purpose.
Dropping the loop over the proper grip, he left the
wheel long enough to get the flashlight from its bulkhead bracket. Returning, he brought the *Nereid* back on
course, and then jumped for the door that led into the
forward compartment. He had only a few seconds to open
the door, swing the light around for a very quick inspec-
tion, and get back to the controls. And a few seconds were
all he needed to see that the glass was gone from one
of the ports . . . the sea came shooting in every time the
bow dropped, and there was more than a foot of water
on the deck.

He staggered back to the wheel and sat there wondering what to do. The cruiser could not be left uncontrolled
long enough for him to try to repair the damage; that
would be a quick and certain end. But, left as it was,
the *Nereid* was slowly sinking.

More out of habit and reflex than conscious effort,
Kip continued to steer. He did not really see or feel
what he was doing, and neither was he very aware of
life being near to an end. He was far too spent and too
defeated to grasp that much of reality. All he could think

of and wonder was *why* . . . why had those people thrown rocks at the whale? It was so long ago . . .

And then there was a blinding, powerful beam of light that stabbed through wind and rain, and swinging around, settled on the *Nereid.*

CHAPTER 19

That sharp line of incandescence, and the brilliance bathing the cruiser, was not something Kip could understand. Not immediately. He was long miles at sea and caught within the growing fury of a hurricane; where in such a time did a light belong?

Its source came closer. When it was less than a hundred yards away, he saw that the light, like his own, twisted and gyrated with the heaving of that wind-torn sea. The thought occurred, then, that it was another vessel in distress, caught as his was by the storm's sudden change in direction, its coming to life again. But he could do nothing for them, nor they for him . . . not in that watery inferno. Anne would have her way, and the best they could do was keep each other's dying company.

Kip settled back into those things that were immediate to him. Clearly, the *Nereid* would not last much longer. Heavy in the bow and settling, it was too often taking sea over the forward deck, now. And this, of course, meant that water was coming into the forward compartment just as frequently . . . a vicious cycle to speed her settling.

Potter's body was still lying where he had left it—motionless, silent, face frozen in some kind of troubled repose. He should have come alone—should have insisted on it. But who could ever argue with the likes of William

Potter? Kip supposed that if he himself had not under-
taken the task of rescuing the whale from so-called hu-
manity, the old man would not have waited much beyond their quarreling to do something about it. Potter
was a gruff and practical man, wise to the realities of
life and sea. But in these realities he found much to
love. And the sea, for all its cruelty, and the whales he
saw as angels, were part of what he loved. Because he
had wandered and searched in the rain, Anne had remained an unknown and unexpected part of his gamble.
But, yes, Potter would have wanted to do something,
and that was the only good thing about his being there.

As for himself, Kip could not quite make the connection with dying. He supposed he was frightened, but
he was too tired to shake and too tired to cry and too
tired to be anything more than bewildered by the idea
of coming to an end and not existing any more.

And what would his mother do? In all this confusing,
hurtling rush of events, Kip had not thought of it before.
What would she do? Between Korean hills and dark,
engulfing sea, she would be alone. A boy had thrown
a rock . . .

It did not make much sense; none of it did.

The *Nereid* shuddered badly, then. Sea came exploding over the bow to slam against the cabin and go
shrieking through the superstructure. For a long moment, the other light was lost to him . . . and when it
came streaming, flickering back into view, Kip realized
that the cruiser was not answering as before. The angle
could be seen in the light, the pronounced listing to port.
Time was short, now.

At this moment, anticipating the worst and not knowing exactly how it would happen, Kip was alarmed to hear one sound begin in the midst of that whole chorus of howling, thundering sounds—begin and take on an insistent rhythm, a steady beat that bore no relation to the measured chaos of the sea. But when nothing immediate came of it, he returned to apathy and waiting, and remembered the day the bell buoy rang out of time with the bay.

The pounding grew louder and more insistent, and Kip could almost swear that somewhere beneath the wind he could hear voices calling to him—the way they had to Nancy Makem. Unnerved by it, he involuntarily turned to look behind him, and barely saw, in the edge of the other light, two faces mouthing inaudible words at him!

It was then, and only then, that the real significance of the light and the other vessel began to reach him. With a cry, he threw himself out of the seat and struggled across the cabin to yank the boat hook away from the door. Men and water came bursting in, and Kip found himself being pulled and half-carried outside, and being all but thrown over the side . . . into waiting arms that reached from a smaller boat.

He was not aware of much after that. The boat remained clear until the two men who had boarded the *Nereid* appeared again carrying Potter. The man on the tiller skillfully brought the boat in close once more to take them off, and quickly pulled away from there to follow a wildly pitching beam of light. And there in that crazy, screaming dark, with rough hands holding him gently, Kip lost touch with the world for a little while . . .

They sat around him in the crew's mess, coastguards-men of the cutter *Wiscasset*. Having taken his clothes to the ship's laundry for drying, and wrapped him in a wool blanket, these men who seemed little older than Kip proceeded to fill him with endless amounts of hot choco-late. They knew that he had towed a whale to sea. But they also wanted to know if, as scuttlebutt had it, he had commandeered a million-dollar yacht to do it. The men who had taken him off the *Nereid* soon scotched that rumor, but questions kept coming, and it was a little while before he could get his breath and start thinking of a few himself.

One of the first things he learned was that Potter was not dead. But it was not until *Wiscasset*'s skipper, a redheaded commander named Murphy, came down from the bridge to talk to him that he learned the old man's condition.

"It's pneumonia, Kip," Murphy said. "That and ex-haustion. But the doc told me that he shot your friend full of holes with a hypodermic, and that with a lot of rest he'll be up and around in a couple of weeks."

"With him unconscious like that, I thought . . ." Kip began.

"I know. And he's still pretty much out of it, but he'll be all right. We'll transfer him to the hospital as soon as we make base."

"When will that be?"

"Sometime tomorrow. Tonight, of course, we have to keep watch for shipping in distress. But it's also for our own safety. We need to go farther out, try to swing around the worst of Anne, and come in behind her. She's hitting the coast now. It's going to be bad, and it's just not the place for us. I'm sorry. I know you're anxious to get home."

Kip managed a tired grin. "I don't mind. We're alive . . . and I'm not in a hurry to go home after losing that cruiser. But could you get word to my mother . . ."

The skipper put an arm around the boy for support. "Let's get you to a bunk, where you can sleep—steady as she goes—all right? Your mother knows you're safe. We radioed the base a short while ago. A man there managed to reach her by phone before the lines started going down. As for the cruiser . . ."

Kip groaned as he staggered down a narrow, heaving passageway. Now that he had nothing else to worry him, the thought of the *Nereid* was overwhelming.

"You heard," Murphy said, "that Terrence Wilcox called the base and reported what you had done?"

"No . . . how did he find out?"

"His boy. Spying on you, I guess. But he saw the whole thing and ran home to tell papa, and . . ."

"And papa really blew his lid!"

"He sure did . . . here, this looks like an unassigned bunk. Get yourself settled and I'll strap you in so you won't be rolling out all night long."

They had reached the crew's quarters, but he had only a quick glimpse of the compartment and of the off-duty watch who were reading or sleeping. Curiosity was not enough to keep him on his feet.

"I guess I'm really in for it . . . Wilcox, I mean."

"He has the right to be a very angry man, Kip, and I'd be lying if I said you weren't going to get a double-barreled blast of it when you reach home. Before he even opens his mouth, you're going to get scorched enough to wish you were somewhere else."

"But . . . couldn't you have towed *Nereid* back?"

"She was too far gone. We would've had to stop the water from coming in, and pump her out. There wasn't time for that."

"The whale . . . I had no other way of doing it. But I was going to bring her back!" Kip tried to sit up.

"Hold still," Murphy told him and brought the strap across. "Of course you intended to bring her back! It didn't work out that way, though, and this is a fact you have to face. Getting all lathered up about it isn't going to help. Now, listen to me. You're going to find an angry man. But I know Terry, and so I can also tell you that you'll find him a reasonable man under all that shouting."

"I don't see how."

"Well, for one thing, the cruiser was fully insured. And for another, Terry knows as well as I do that he probably would have lost her tonight anyway. There's very little chance that Anne wouldn't have destroyed her at the dock. But more than that, Kip, he does know your circumstances. When his boy told him about the *Nereid*, Terry put two and two together—because of all the fuss about the whale and the way his son had been acting— and got the boy to spill the whole story. So while he's angry at you for taking the cruiser instead of asking for help, he's also aware that his son is at least partly responsible."

"He talked to you . . ." Kip said, sleepily.

"Yes, when he called the base. A few minutes before we finished taking on fuel and put out to sea. That's all

I can tell you, except for one thing. I gather from what Terry said that all of this is having a remarkable effect on Farley. You might not know him when you get back."

"Don't want to," Kip muttered.

"I know. Spoiled rotten. But what with a very black eye and thinking he might've committed murder by causing two people to go sailing off into a hurricane . . . well, I was told that the boy was watching everything with one eye and being unusually quiet. So . . . can you sleep now?"

"Yes."

"Then I'll see you in the morning."

In those final moments before sleep, Kip stopped listening to Anne and thought about the killer whale—remembered how it had all begun. It was strange, and unexpected, to feel no sadness now, or any real sense of loss. The old man had tried to tell him about the whale and a different world—about things having a scheme, a pattern, and of there being no way of departing from it for long. And he supposed Potter was right. But he had not come to that limit to learn or see by himself; the cruelty of people had made short time shorter. How, then, could it be accepted so easily? Maybe it was the kind of love that Harper had talked about. And maybe it was easy only because he was without a choice. Kip closed his eyes and no longer questioned any of it. All that mattered now was that the whale was in a better place.

Somewhere deep and far from the storm . . .

J. Allan Bosworth began writing while still a radioman aboard the USS *Missouri*. World War II had just ended, and the ship was on her long voyage home. A native Californian, he returned to San Francisco and took a job at the *Chronicle*. Ten years later, having published two novels and a few dozen short stories, he left the newspaper to begin writing on a full-time basis. He and his wife and two daughters now live in Salem, Virginia. Mr. Bosworth's last book for young people, *All the Dark Places*, was chosen by *School Library Journal* as one of the fifty best books of 1968.